I0531432

Dedicated to Melissa Burton

~~*~~

Special Thanks and Gratitude

to

Beverly Blankenbaker, Callie Mulrooney,

Shannon Burton, Robin Smedley, and Karen Block

Small Town Christmas

MAGDALENA SCOTT

~~*~~

Trade Paperback Release: November 2014

ISBN 978-0-9862118-1-2

~~*~~

Digital Release: November 2014

ISBN 978-0-9862118-0-5

Jewel Box Books

www.jewelboxbooks.com

CHAPTER ONE

There was only one thing that could have brought me back to Serendipity, Indiana, and that was the Osborne house. As a youngster riding all over town on my bike, I'd thought it was surely the most beautiful house in the world. My senior year in high school I attended an event there—an event that changed the direction of my life. The day I drove out of town in my first car, intending never to return, I shed a tear or two at the thought of never seeing that house again. I told myself those tears had nothing at all to do with Jim Standish, or his part in my last experience at the Osborne house.

Years later I made the huge mistake of telling my

best girlfriends that the house was the only thing that could get me back to Serendipity. We all laughed about it. But when the Osbornes decided to move to Florida for good and not just snowbird as a lot of Serendipity folks did, my friend Alice called me.

"Mel, guess what? There's a 'for sale' sign in the front yard of the Osborne house."

A shock ran through me like static electricity on a cold wintry day.

"Remember what you said?"

"Sure, I remember." Why do I tell girlfriends stuff that might come back to bite me? "You know, if things were different for me here, I'd be tempted. The housing market's picked up. Business is great. I can't imagine I could have much of a career in real estate down there. So, you know…"

"Okay. Wanted to tell you, just in case." The conversation went someplace entirely different after that, thank goodness. It had been less than a blip on the big radar screen of my life.

"So, how's Matthew?" she asked when I'd probably been talking too much about my job.

"Great. Absolutely wonderful. What did I ever do without him?"

"Work. Even more hours than you do now."

"Well, true."

"Mel, we need a girls' day, soon. Can you manage it?"

We discussed schedules and Alice took the job of contacting the other girls. It made sense because they're in the same town, and—well, she doesn't really seem to have much else going on. She organizes us for things like this—finds a fun place for lunch and some shopping, somewhere between Fort Wayne, where I was living, and Serendipity, which is way the other end of Indiana. Plus it's way the other end of the spectrum, quality of life-wise. Poor old Serendipity, where nothing ever happens but everybody's always talking about it.

Matthew scooted into the room in his favorite footed jammies, rubbing sleep out of his eyes. "Mommy, who was on the phone?"

"Sorry my call woke you up, Sweetie. That was my friend, Alice."

He raised his arms and I picked him up and started walking around talking softly. I almost made the mistake of asking if he remembered Alice, but that would have been stupid because he'd have started thinking about it and become *more* awake instead of drowsy. I have to think about parenting stuff more than some people do, I think. Maybe because I came to motherhood a little late and all alone. Plus my own parents sure hadn't set a good example of how to raise children.

Matthew had brought his piece of blanket with him and tucked it under his cheek, relaxing on my shoulder. I started singing the silly song I made up as a lullaby— a real repetitive tune and boring words —that always works at night. Sometimes I almost put myself to sleep.

But this was morning and I needed to get moving. I laid my son back in his little bed shaped like a semi-truck, made sure he was sound asleep, and retrieved the nursery monitor before I hit the shower. I usually have coffee before I shower, but today I was running a little late because of Alice's phone call. And I didn't need caffeine. My mind was whirling with pictures and memories of the Osborne house, of my girlfriends in Serendipity, and the sweetness of life in a small town. We'd had an idyllic childhood for the most part, back in the day when life was more simple than scary. Sure I'd love to raise Matthew in a similar environment, but Serendipity isn't a place to move to, if you need to make a living. Young people with initiative move out of town as soon as they can, as I had done a couple of decades ago. The town had lost more industry than it had gained in the last several years and was basically headed down the tubes. Most likely the Osborne house would sit empty, unsold, and the owners would end up renting it out.

Too bad, but not my problem. My life was coming along very nicely, thank you very much.

****

A few days later I watched Matthew play at the park near our apartment. He and I had a standing play date with some kids from his preschool every Saturday morning. It was good for him to be able to run wild for a little while, since our apartment didn't have loads of room for that type of activity. I always brought my laptop and used the play date time to catch up on work. The other moms were lots younger and busy talking about husbands or boyfriends or the latest fashion. I didn't have anything to add to that conversation, nor anything to gain from it either.

My cell phone rang. This time it was my friend Francie, just re-stating the fact that the house was for sale. I steeled myself not to care.

"And hey—did you know the Parkers are retiring and closing their office?"

"Parkers?"

"Parker Realty. You know. The biggest real estate office in the county."

"Um, no. When did this happen?" *And why does it feel like a sign to me?*

"It's been in the works for a while, I guess. There's been talk, but I got the official word from Maude Parker yesterday in the grocery line. She's excited to retire. They have kids all over the country, and can travel—"

"So who's going to buy the business?"

"Maude said they're working on it. They don't really want to sell to somebody from out of town, you know. Most of the real estate places around are just satellites, not really local. She said selling to that kind of owner just feels wrong." She paused. "Alice called me about a get-together. I think we're shooting for some time next month. Everybody's busy right now."

"Do you have the number?"

"Number?"

"The Parkers' number, Francie." Why did she keep changing the subject? "Home phone, not the business." I started pawing through Matthew's backpack for something to write the number on. It was ludicrous to even make the contact, but if I was going to, I wanted to go right to the owners, via a more personal channel. I mean, if they had the inclination to sell to someone they knew, who was I to question it?

"I can get it for you, Mel. Mom may have Maude's number. I'll text it to you."

She sent it to me that day or the next, but having come to my senses in the interim, I didn't call. The idea of owning my own business had been a silly idea. I was established and successful, and Matthew and I were happy.

Then the final shoe dropped. This particular size twelve, Italian-leather loafer belonged to the owner of the real estate agency where I worked. In order to focus best on the agency's core mission, there was to be a redistribution of human resources. Translation: The dude's new girlfriend was coming onboard and I was on my way out.

I may be a little slow on the uptake, but I can tell when fate is kicking me in the rear. At this point I could try to keep my job by whatever means available—could be ugly. Or I could look for something similar in the area. Or I could just take door number three—Serendipity, Indiana, the old hometown I had tried so hard to put in the past. If I'd only had myself to consider, I might have chosen another option. But Matthew made everything in my life different.

CHAPTER TWO

"Mommy, I need to potty."

I looked in the rearview mirror. "Matthew, we just stopped ten minutes ago and did that, remember? We're almost there, Sweetie."

"Okay." He huffed out a big sigh and pulled another storybook out of his backpack. He propped the book onto the arm rest of his car seat and smoothed his blanket a few times with one hand. Dear little Matthew. It was a sudden upheaval, and this trip was wearing on him.

"Sweetie, you're going to love our new house. It's big and pretty with lots of windows."

Matthew met my eyes in the rearview mirror. "Tell me about my room, Mommy. Tell me it's gonna have trucks and soft carpet."

"Yes, it will. Right now, it's a nice room, but when we get the trucks painted on the walls, it will be even better. All your friends will wish they had a terrific room like that."

"Only I don't have friends, Mommy. We drived away from my friends."

I stared at the road, unwilling to see my son's expression.

"You'll make lots of new friends in Serendipity, Matthew."

"I don't like Sarahdippty. It's a girl name."

"Not Sarah, Sweetie. Serendipity. It's one really long word that isn't about a girl or a boy. Serendipity is a word that means good luck. Isn't that a fun name for a town?"

"They should call it Good Luck Town."

I could tell by his tone that Matthew was getting sleepy. I slid a CD of soft jazz into the player, and he was asleep in a few minutes. By the time he woke up we should be at our destination.

I knew the big house on Main Street would be perfect for us. I had made sure zoning would allow me to use a portion of the house for my real estate office. Even if I eventually needed an assistant, which I anticipated, there was lots of square footage for a grand home—the home I'd wanted all my life. It had taken a long while, but the house—and pretty much everything about the move—had dropped into my lap without much effort from me. Maybe the biggest perk was that I'd be able to walk down the streets of Serendipity, Indiana, as someone who mattered…even though for years I had tried not caring about that.

It would have been obvious to me even without road signs that we were nearing my hometown because of the change in terrain. I'd lived in the Chicago area and northern Indiana ever since leaving Serendipity, and, especially early on, I'd missed the rolling hills of southern Indiana. Up north, the roads are flat and straight and actually meet at right angles—a great help if you're driving around a lot in areas you're not familiar with. Not so in the southern part of the state.

You could start driving east on a road and a mile later, there's a horseshoe curve and you're staring into the sunset, due west. Going for a Sunday drive, you could easily end up someplace you didn't expect at all. That was the roads, but also when you paid attention, it was just the way life tended to work in Serendipity.

I took the exit off I-65, and said a silent *thank you* that Matthew hadn't stirred. Suddenly, on this familiar two-lane state highway I had traveled a million times in my youth, I was anxious about my decision to move back, and what kind of welcome we might receive. However, given that I had already burned my bridges behind me, it was a little late for second thoughts.

I wiped my sweaty palms one at a time on the fabric of my designer jeans, and concentrated on breathing calmly. Moving back here would work out. I would make sure of it.

Twenty minutes later, I slowed the SUV to a crawl at the Serendipity city limits. Off to the right was a new-looking medical plaza. That certainly hadn't existed when I left. Just across the road from the new medical plaza stood the big white farm house where one of my high school classmates had grown up. Black Angus cattle, not impressed one way or the other about Serendipity's progress, calmly grazed in the large field near the house, just as their ancestors had done.

The town had always been boring and way behind the times. That was part of why I'd moved away, of course. I came to the stop light and had to wait. A few blocks away to the left, the stately courthouse was visible. I looked forward to the first time Matthew would see the castle-like building, but that was for another day. Right now, I was too tired from driving and trying to keep Matthew entertained along the way.

The light changed to green and I turned right onto Main Street and a hundred yards later, left into our driveway.

"Are we there yet?" Matthew asked thickly.

"We sure are, Sweetie. We sure are."

I sat for a moment looking at our home. The big square house was perfect as ever, newly painted white and with forest green shutters that matched the roof on the deep-set front porch. So beautiful, just as it had always been.

"Is this our house, Mommy?"

I hurried to unbuckle my son from his car seat. "Yes. Isn't it beautiful? We'll be so happy here, Matthew."

"Big. It is so *big!*" He stared in awe. "Can I have a dog?"

I laughed nervously. Where had that question come from? "Let's go in and see the house."

I took his hand and led him to the side door at the driveway, lifted a small concrete figurine of a boy and girl kissing, and plucked the key from its hiding place. All the paperwork had been taken care of by email and snail-mail, and the realtor had told me where to find the key. I immediately worked it onto my ring. No way would I permanently leave a key out for anyone to find. That was one facet of small town life I'd never buy into. That and simply leaving doors unlocked. Ridiculous to do such things these days, for sure.

We entered the side door. I found a light switch and flipped it. A large chandelier filled the room with light.

"Ooh." said Matthew. He let go of my hand and

walked directly under the dining room chandelier, staring up at it, awestruck. "Shiny."

"Melissa. Hey, I know you're in there."

In a few seconds I was caught up in a tight hug.

"Carla. How did you know we were here? I hadn't even had a chance to text or call."

Carla Standish took a half step back but had a death grip on my upper arms.

"You *have* been gone a long time." she laughed, her dark eyes sparkling. "Out-of-county license plate on a black Acura SUV turning into the drive of the old Osborne house which, according to the sales disclosure listings in the paper a week ago, was sold to the mysterious MM Investments. Information moves fast in Serendipity—faster than ever. I knew you were here before you did, honey."

Small town stuff. It would take a while to get used to again. I pulled my dear friend into another hug and then releasing Carla, swept Matthew up into my arms.

"Carla, you remember Matthew." He uncertainly looked around for his blanket which he'd left in the car. He started smoothing my long hair instead, a motion that helped calm him.

Carla looked stunned for a second, but then stuck out her hand. "Matthew, I haven't seen you since you were just a little guy. Wow, you've changed now you're growing up." She tipped her head and smiled, pulling his hand into hers to shake it. "Even more handsome. I know your mommy is really proud of you."

I nuzzled my son's soft cheek. "Sweetie, Carla and I were best friends when we were kids."

Matthew's brow wrinkled as he tried to imagine us as children.

"Carla, do you have a dog?"

"Dog? Nope, but my parents—uh, my mom—has a great dog. Her name is Daisy. Would you like to meet her?"

"Yes. Can she come visit us?" He looked from Carla to me. "Mommy, can Daisy come here?"

He had stopped smoothing my hair, so I leaned down and set him on the floor. He seemed heavier today than yesterday even, he was growing so quickly. "Goodness, Sweetie, you're getting to be such a big boy."

He nodded soberly. "So probly I should get a dog. Right, Mommy?"

Carla beamed down at him. "Matthew, you're a busy boy, aren't you?"

He looked uncertain and stepped a little behind me. "Maybe."

"Hey, don't get me wrong. Busy is good. You ask a lot of questions, I bet."

"No bet," I replied.

Carla looked deeply into my eyes for a moment. "Let's look around your house, Matthew. Then we'll make sure you and Mommy have a good dinner. How would that be?"

"Good." He stepped out from behind me. "Chicken nuggets?"

Carla rolled her eyes but smiled. "Hmm. That might have to wait 'til another time."

I just wanted to throw myself onto my huge leather sofa, eat a bunch of carbs, and drink wine. The fact that none of those things were currently in the house just made me want them more.

Thank God for reinforcements. Carla's sister Francie and their mom, Lillian Standish, arrived then, and right behind them was Alice.

"Housewarming party," Francie announced. She was carrying grocery bags that looked promising.

"How long was your drive today?" Lillian asked as she hugged me.

"Eight hours when you include stops to—you know, potty and have a picnic and watch bugs on the sidewalk."

She smiled, maybe remembering when her own boys were small. Lillian had changed so much in the last few months, since her husband died. She was still lovely, but carried an aura of sadness. Even when she smiled, she looked sad.

Alice propped the side door open and brought in more grocery bags. "We considered taking you out to eat, but thought you might enjoy just unwinding here."

"Sounds like heaven. Not that I have furniture yet—"

"We'll make do," said Carla, who handed Matthew a bag to carry. "But hey, before we eat, let's have the grand tour. I want to see this place. It's been years."

"For me, too. A little scary buying it sight unseen." I'd known the Osbornes would leave it in immaculate shape, but also remembered the last time I'd been in the house. That fiasco was emblazoned on my brain.

We trooped through the elegant dining room into the big sunny kitchen.

"Wow. This looks brand new, doesn't it?" Carla ran a hand along the red granite countertop. "Gorgeous. New cabinets, state-of-the-art appliances—"

"Mommy?" Matthew had pulled his hand out of Carla's and was trying to unlatch the back door. "Can I go outside?"

"We can walk out for a minute, Sweetie." I was excited for him to see what was out there, but a bit apprehensive for myself.

The grocery bags were unceremoniously plopped onto the beautiful countertop and pitchers of tea stuck into the fridge.

"Oh my goodness. I'd forgotten about this," Francie whispered.

A beautiful in-ground pool lined in mosaic tile, an

elegant deck surrounding it, complete with a pool house for changing, took up the area between the back of the house and the fence on the property line. There were large terra cotta containers that could hold flowers in the summer, but now they were empty, as was the pool.

"Amazing, isn't it?" I'd been imagining pool parties for Matthew and his friends, and lazy weekends soaking up rays, or reading thick novels under an umbrella as I watched Matthew paddling back and forth on a big inflatable raft. It would be perfect! The pain and sadness I had associated with this pool for years could be left behind, replaced with happy memories, love and laughter.

"My goodness, that's a lot of swimming pool." Lillian looked around. "No backyard at all?"

"That's part of the beauty of it. No maintenance."

"No yard to cut," Alice corrected. "The pool will be a lot of maintenance. I'm surprised the Osbornes kept it up all these years. It's even prettier than I remember."

I hugged myself in delight, watching Matthew explore the deck levels and try to peer between the boards of the tall white fence that surrounded the lot. "I'll hire somebody to deal with the pool, if I need to. We'll love it."

"Cabana boy?" Carla nudged Alice and laughed. Shaking my head and laughing too, I walked to the pool house.

I tried the door of the pool house but it was locked. "In theory, the deck furniture is in there. They were supposed to leave things like that. It was part of the agreement." I shrugged and took Matthew's hand. "We can have picnics out here in the summer, Sweetie. The key was to be left in the kitchen on a hook. I'll check in a few, and we can come back outside later. Let's look at the rest of the house."

We filed up the back stairway which was beautiful hardwood and pleasantly squeaky with age. A central hallway ran the length of the house, with four huge bedrooms opening off of it. The master suite had a walk-in closet, glorious bathroom done all in black, white, and chrome, with double sinks, a separate bath tub and shower, bidet, and toilet. Two other bedrooms shared a bath between them, and the fourth bedroom, across the hall from the master suite, had its own bathroom, smaller than the master but with similarly luxurious appointments. The hall and bedrooms were carpeted in white, and the secondary bathrooms were tiled in bright, happy colors.

The ladies said little but took it all in, eyes wide. Matthew repeatedly exclaimed, "Wow. It's so *big*."

It was indeed. Big and beautiful. Nearly palatial by Serendipity standards. It was even more wonderful than when I had been here years ago and fallen hard—in love with the house, and out of love with the handsome quarterback of the Serendipity Pirates football team.

We went down the front stairs, which were also carpeted in white and led to the massive living room.

"Good grief. You could hold church in this living room," said Carla. "It's fabulous."

Matthew ran to the window seat and climbed into it. "Mommy, I can sit here and watch trucks."

"That's fun." I walked over and looked out the window too. There were nearly as many pickup trucks as cars driving slowly along. "I never understood where all the traffic was going. Not as if there's anything happening in Serendipity."

"Yet you're moving back."

Startled, I turned to Alice. "Sorry. I didn't realize I'd said that out loud."

"Yep." Carla tipped her head and a dangly diamond earring swayed with the movement. "I've said it before, but I'll repeat myself. I'm thrilled to have you back in town, Melissa. I just hope you won't regret it." She looked toward her mom, but Lillian was enthralled with watching Matthew.

I swiveled away again, walked over and opened the door to a wood-paneled den. "Here's my office. Some of the old guard are gone now—people who were in the real estate business when we were kids. People who had a lot of respect in the community. It's the ideal time for an ambitious, knowledgeable realtor to come in and set up shop." I lowered my voice and nodded toward Matthew who was still sitting in the window seat a few yards away, chattering excitedly to Lillian.

"Plus next fall Matthew will start kindergarten. I don't want him in some giant elementary school where nobody knows him. I want him to have the start we did—with teachers who know us and don't mind calling home if there's a need." I shook my head and forced a smile, frustrated that I felt like crying. "Sorry. Nervous exhaustion."

Carla took my hand and Alice and Francie drew close too.

"Matthew is darling. It's been tough raising him alone, I know," said Carla "Now you're here, some of us can help you. That will be good for everybody. It's the kind of thing Serendipity folks do well."

Francie smiled sadly. "I guess part of wanting the house has to do with Jim."

"No…not really. I've always loved this house. It's so big and substantial looking. It always looked to me, as a kid, as if this house could withstand anything—like a lighthouse perched on a rocky cliff. Maybe you remember the house I grew up in and the way our family interacted."

The girls winced at that. Not a happy memory for anyone involved.

"So as a kid I looked at this place and imagined that if I lived here, I'd be happier. Safer." I noticed the skeptical smirks on my friends' faces. "Of course, the last night I was here was a nasty turning point in my life. It'll be cathartic for me to own the place where that happened, you know? Kind of—physically taking control of the past and making it positive instead of painful like it's been up until now." They nodded soberly. "So I wanted it for both those reasons." I winked. "Plus it's gorgeous."

We all laughed.

"You're very brave to take this big step, Mel." Francie looked worried, and I smiled at her.

"I have a lot riding on this move, in every possible sense of that phrase. I've made some big commissions in the last couple of years, so have a bit of a financial cushion for now. I know it will work out, but I'm still nervous."

The rest of the house tour—sitting room and powder room—was accomplished without Matthew's presence, as he seemed glued to the window seat, his eyes intent on each truck as it passed.

"Furniture should arrive in a couple of days, but 'til then, we'll be a little uncomfortable."

Carla, Francie, and Alice mobilized in the kitchen.

"But at least there will be food. One pool-side picnic coming up."

"Oops. Forgot cups." Alice had made pitchers of sweet tea and had a bag of ice, but there wasn't a genteel way to drink it.

"Matthew and I can walk down to the corner and buy some plastic cups," Carla offered. "Okay?" He seemed to have accepted everyone so quickly, but I was surprised at his willingness to leave the window seat. Then again, it meant walking along the sidewalk so he could watch the trucks and hear them better. "While we're doing that, you can dig out the deck furniture."

We located the pool house key, and Francie and I pulled the brightly colored Adirondack-style chairs out of the crowded pool house and wiped them all down, Alice and Lillian set out the food and paper plates in my beautiful new kitchen.

It was late in the year to eat outdoors, but with the sun shining on the pretty furniture set around the gorgeous pool, it was festive and inviting. I wanted the house to always be that for us and for our friends—a place known for its warmth and hospitality. Portions of my former life in Serendipity made that a challenge, but I was certain I was up to it.

CHAPTER THREE

Carla and Matthew returned shortly with plastic cups and a surprise.

"Mommy! Mr. Jim comed to see us. He haves a big *truck*."

Mr. Jim?

I met them in the living room. Carla carrying the plastic bag with red cups poking out the top, and Matthew, his face beaming, holding the hand of the one guy I had dreaded running into.

"Hi, Jim. Long time." It felt like a hundred years—or maybe fifteen minutes.

"Mel. This is quite a surprise." He looked past me

to his other sister, his mother, and our friend Alice. "I see I'm the last one in my family to know you're back in town."

"Mr. Jim haves a big truck," Matthew said more softly this time, looking up at me and to Jim and back again. Obviously, the strain between me and this man was apparent to him.

"What color truck is it, Matthew?" I crouched down and held his hands.

"Blue," he whispered, his eyes wide.

"Wow. Blue is Matthew's favorite color of truck, Jim. Did you know that?" I looked up at him from Matthew's side.

"So he told me. Um, so you're MM Investments? I saw it in the sales disclosures in the paper."

"Yes. This is a business venture for me."

"Ah. Completely impersonal?"

"Yes. Completely."

"Most people don't come back to Serendipity for business reasons." He smiled thinly. "Most people, once they leave, don't ever move back to town."

"As was my intention, in fact. Things just kind of

fell into place for this move. Matthew and I are excited to be here."

"Are you now?"

"Yes."

"You don't look all that happy about it, Mel." He touched a finger to the little cleft in my chin, a touch that had been intimate and endearing back in the day. With great restraint, I kept myself from swatting his hand away.

"I may not look happy *now*, but I bet I looked lots happier before you got here," I whispered.

"Food, people!" Francie's yell wasn't exactly tactful, but at least it broke the tension of the moment.

"Can Mr. Jim be at the picnic?"

"Um…" Jim and I both started to speak.

"Probably Mr. Jim needs to go someplace else *right now*," Carla suggested.

Lillian came in and took Jim by one hand and Matthew by the other.

"Mr. Jim is my little boy, Matthew," she said sweetly, gently steering them in the direction of the kitchen. "His daddy and I taught him very good manners." She sent Jim a warning glance. "He works hard at his job, so I'm sure he's hungry for dinner. But afterward he'll need to leave right away. Isn't that right, Jim?"

"Sure is. Thanks, Mom." He looked around at me. "Thanks for inviting me to stay, Mel. I appreciate it."

He appreciated the fact that I hadn't invited, and wouldn't have invited, and that if it had been just him and me, I'd have gladly kicked him out. But this was my first day back in town, I was tired, and there were witnesses. I could play nice just this one time.

"Mr. Jim let me drive his truck," Matthew told Lillian as they disappeared into the kitchen.

"Translation: Sit in it, with the key out, hold the steering wheel, and make engine noises," Carla whispered at my ear. "Matthew asked, and in Jim's defense, I don't know how anybody could have looked into that little face and said, 'no.'"

I counted silently to ten. What an interesting introduction to Serendipity it had been so far.

****

Two days later when the moving truck arrived, I was as excited as Matthew. His big deal was having his truck-shaped bed set up in his new room with the freshly painted trucks on the walls. Thanks to my girlfriends that had taken very little time to accomplish and looked great. But where Matthew's excitement was his sleeping environment, mine was setting up my first-ever, solo real estate office. Sure, I'd had a work space in our apartment, but this was a completely different experience.

This time I was on my own, one hundred percent. I was thrilled beyond imagination and scared to death at the same time. Kind of like having a relationship with Jim Standish. Except that had been thrilling, scary, and doomed to disaster. I could do without the last component on this new phase of my life.

The moving guys were pleasant enough, but seriously unhappy about my choice in office furniture. I had lucked into an estate sale just days after making the decision to move. The furniture was antique, of great quality, and heavy as lead. The dark polished wood had "class" and "respectability" written all over it. Figuratively, that is. The guys had to shift the huge desk a couple of times until I was sure the light would hit just right over my shoulder when I was working. I would have preferred to do all this setting up completely on my own but there was no way I could budge any of the pieces without help.

Fortunately for the movers, the office was their main hassle. The living room had only the big leather sectional and coffee table, a couple of lamps, and a brass hall tree by the front door. My dining room table and chairs were dwarfed by the size of their new space, and I realized I'd need to upgrade soon. Our previous kitchen had been tiny in comparison, so there weren't a lot of boxes to be carried into the new one. Beds for Matthew and myself, our chests of drawers, and clothes, and the movers were out of there.

Yeah, I'd bought a huge house and only had furniture for about one tenth of it, but it turned out that I liked the open feeling of all that empty space. Our apartment had been cozy, but this looked minimalist with the very same contents, and the two empty bedrooms upstairs made for some awkward conversations.

"Mommy, my dog can sleep in this room," Matthew would say, and then walk across the hall. "My new brother can sleep in this room." Then he would smile that heart-melting smile that had yielded him a few minutes 'driving' Jim's truck, among other things.

Well, his puppy-dog eyes weren't going to get him a brother. And the jury was still out on the dog. I wasn't sure I could handle the complication right now.

CHAPTER FOUR

"Ms. Singer, okay if I go now?" Emily stood in the doorway to my office, her jacket in one hand and cell phone in the other, texting with one thumb but looking at me. "Matthew's in the window seat." She smiled and tipped her head toward him.

Of course he was. That's where he preferred to spend most of his waking time, it seemed. I was super busy networking with the local business people and other realtors in town. I didn't have any time to waste in building my business, if I was going to prosper. The Parkers' retirement was not only a windfall to me but to others as well, as homeowners were faced with the perceived choice of which second-best realtor to choose to sell their property. I had also been lucky to find Emily, a nice high school grad who needed a local job, to stay with Matthew while I worked.

"Same time tomorrow, right Emily?"

"Yep." She blew a big bubble and popped it. "Sure thing."

"Weather's supposed to be nice. It should be a great day for a trip to the park. You two could even walk there. I know Matthew would love playing on the swings. He and I went last Saturday, and he really enjoyed it."

"Oh." Emily's smile faded. "Um, see you tomorrow."

She turned toward Matthew. "Hey, I'm leaving, Matthew. See you tomorrow, okay?"

"'kay. Bye, Em'ly."

I needed to talk to Emily about things. She seemed to give in to every request Matthew made. Emily and Matthew walked to the pizza shop for lunch, even if I had made lunch preparations the night before. Emily and Matthew took a daily stroll to the ice cream place a few blocks in the other direction, and Emily drove him to the park, which was a good idea, and the grocery, which was not. I was appalled to find large quantities of junk food in my kitchen cabinets. It needed to stop, and when Emily arrived tomorrow morning, I would take her aside and explain again what was expected of her.

I didn't like dealing with conflict like this. Growing up, my family had been so full of conflict, I had fled to my friends' homes as much as possible. I spent a lot of nights with the Campbells—Alice's family, or the Standishes—Carla and Francie's. And after high school I had taken my scholarship papers and escaped. Forever, I had thought. Funny how forever doesn't always last as long as you expect.

Emily's departure each afternoon signaled the end of my work day until after Matthew went to sleep. There was no way I could concentrate on work and be sure he was okay. It was a good thing that I had to stop working and spend time with him, because otherwise my Type A personality might have taken over. That person I'd been before—the woman who was wholly consumed by her career—had disappeared when

Matthew was born. The first moment I looked into that tiny red face swaddled in the receiving blanket, I was in love. Time with Matthew was never to be endured. It was to be savored.

"I wanna sit in Mr. Jim's truck, Mommy," he said, when I sat next to him and watched Emily jump into her little red car out front. "Remember he said I could?"

And yet it would be easier to savor our time together, if I had had enough sleep. I was having an awful time the last few days. Matthew still insisted on sleeping with me instead of in his own bed in the fun new room. I didn't want him to be frightened in the big house, so hadn't pushed the issue. He flopped around a lot while he slept, waking me numerous times during the night in spite of it being a queen-size bed. After a couple of weeks of this, plus plenty of sleepless time worrying about establishing the business, I was exhausted and irritable.

"Remember, Mommy," Matthew whined. "My new friend, Mr. Jim.

"Yes, Sweetie. I remember Mr. Jim."

It was completely impossible to forget him, and I'd

tried for a lot of years.

****

The next morning, still sleep deprived, I managed coffee and a shower, but looped my long hair into a knot at the back of my neck because anything else seemed too much effort.

I practiced my speech. *'Emily, we need to talk. I'm not sure how I failed to communicate clearly before, but I have certain expectations regarding Matthew. Um…'*

The phone rang.

"Mommy, can I answer it?"

I narrowly beat his quick little hand and scooped up my cell. "MM Investments." As I listened to the voice on the other end, I felt a rushing in my ears. I don't know how much later Matthew was standing next to me, patting my arm.

"Mommy? Mommy?"

"Oh. Oh, my God, Matthew." I swept him into my arms and held him tight, not able to stop the flow of tears. The caller had been Emily's mother. Emily had been in a terrible car wreck late last night and had been flown to a hospital in Louisville. Both Emily's parents and her siblings were with her now. They had been told by the doctors there was a fifty-fifty chance for the young woman to leave the hospital alive. They didn't know—they didn't know.

It was the first week of November. The weather had chilled. Christmas songs were playing on the radio already. Young, energetic Emily might or might not live to see another Christmas.

I felt horrible. Here I had been, rehearsing a speech to straighten Emily out, and my main complaint was going to be junk food?

The doorbell rang and Matthew was up, racing to answer it. I pushed myself up from the chair I'd slumped into, and followed him.

"Hey, guess what today is, Matthew," said Carla, looking strangely overexcited.

"What?" The child began to nearly dance with enthusiasm. "Birthday?"

"Nope. Better than that. Today is your first visit to our Christmas tree farm."

"Yay! What is it?"

"Oh, Matthew." She looked at me. "*Melissa!* He's never been to a Christmas tree farm?"

"Well, you know, big city…."

"So sad. So very sad. Just a few miles from Serendipity is the very best Christmas tree farm. And it's the best because it's where I grew up."

"You grew up in—Christmas?"

"Well, yes, kind of." Carla winked at him.

"My mom—Miss Lillian—lives there now, in the house where I grew up, and she wants you to come and see her. She likes to bake cookies, but she says cookies are best if she has a good helper. Do you think you could learn to help, Matthew?"

He considered carefully. "I can help. Does she got a truck on her farm?"

"Does she a have a truck? Heavens yes. A truck and some tractors and four wheelers." She held up a hand. "Those are for the grown-ups, and you always have to ask permission to ride with somebody." She kissed the top of Matthew's head and spun him away from her. "How about you go get your jacket and I'll drive you out there?" He was on the move immediately, racing up the front stairs to his room.

Carla lowered her voice. "Honey, we heard about poor Emily. Mom and Francie came up with the idea for Matthew to go out there, at least for today. Mom's looking forward to it, and that's really encouraging for those of us who've seen her struggle to have any enthusiasm for life since Dad died." She cleared her throat. "You don't mind, do you?"

I sagged against her, hugging her close. "Of course, I don't mind. Sounds like a wonderful idea, and I'm so grateful to all of you. Matthew and Lillian will have fun together, and I'll work, and maybe by this evening there will be good news about Emily."

Matthew dashed back down the stairs, clutching one of his favorite little trucks, and dragging his jacket behind him. "Mommy, can Em'ly come with us? I don't want her to be sad."

I helped him put on his jacket, then crouched down in front to zip it. I kissed him and he kissed me back.

"Matthew, I love you so much. Thank you for thinking about Emily." I sniffed back a tear. "She's with her family today, but maybe another time she can go to the farm."

Carla smiled determinedly. "Emily has been getting her Christmas trees from our farm her whole life, Matthew. She'll be glad that you get to see it. Ready now?"

They were gone in an instant, leaving me weak with worry about Emily, and with gratitude for Carla and the Standish family.

CHAPTER FIVE

I turned off the state highway onto Tree Farm Road to retrieve my son. Emily was enduring rehab at a facility in the metro area and doing well, but it would be a long time before she would be able to supervise Matthew. So the one-time event of him spending the day with Lillian Standish had become every weekday at her insistence, and everyone involved seemed happy with the set-up. I still had to cajole her into taking payment at the end of the week, but that was a small thing.

Lillian had so much patience with him, not worrying if he got dirty or spilled something by accident. She treated him as moms of her time had treated their kids, not as concerned about things as I always was. Lillian even let Matthew use a wooden toy truck that had been her husband Harry's and then later Jim's and his brother David's.

That truck was Matthew's favorite thing to play with there, and on sunny days I might pull up and find Lillian standing at her kitchen window watching Matthew play outdoors. He'd be bundled up and loading trimmings from the pine trees onto the wooden truck 'to take Christmas to people.' The nearest grove of trees started a few dozen feet from the back of the house, so Lillian, and sometimes Francie too, watched to be sure he was okay. He'd crawl on his hands and knees driving the truck with Harry's black Lab, Daisy, sitting beside him. A couple of times when I arrived, if I closed the car door quietly and slipped around the side of the house, I'd see Matthew playing like that or standing among the young trees, talking to Daisy. You could watch an exchange between those two, but, of course, none of us asked what their private conversations were. I was grateful Matthew was able to have this type of grandmotherly attention. And I got really good at washing ground-in dirt out of the knees of his jeans.

As I drove along thinking of how well this was all working out for Matthew, I was also encouraged about my business. Today a developer had come to my office and told me about the place he wanted to build in the Serendipity area. It seemed extremely ambitious to expect people to build huge luxurious homes in this small rural community, but he insisted it was a goldmine.

"These are people who are tired of the miserably hot summers and the crime and dirty air of the city, Ms. Singer. These are people who don't mind an hour-plus commute, because when they get home they're in their own kind of nirvana. Picture it." He swung one hand above him. "Big, placid lake, lots of trees everywhere. Large lots, but mowing service provided for them, and paid monthly. Low maintenance, see? So much cool shade and loads of *privacy* which maybe they've never had, if they've always lived in the city. The pricier lots will have their own piers into the lake, and folks can have canoes or those little paddle boat things. Nothing noisy or powerful. It's all about luxury and relaxation." He turned to me, his face near mine as I pictured it too. I blinked a couple of times and stepped back. "Can you see it?" he asked.

"Um. Yes, I think I can, actually. Nice."

"Nice? It's fabulous. Amazing." He spun around and gestured toward Main Street. "Ms. Singer, this development is the best thing that ever happened to this little backwater. Tax base goes up, schools are improved, more people shop in the grocery, buy their jewelry at the little shop on the square. Suddenly, there are more jobs in town, and the quality of life goes way up."

Though I might use the term myself, I didn't like him referring to Serendipity as a backwater. Other than that, what he said sounded good. Potentially good, that is. At this point, his vision was just an idea, but Jared Barnett was quite a salesman. I wasn't easily sold, yet I'd been completely dazzled. *Wow.* Was I losing it, or was it really possible?

"I want a couple hundred acres ideally. Needs to be

close to a state highway, and have lots of beautiful trees, and those rolling hills. And a lake, if you can manage it. We can build a lake if we need to, but it'd be nice if it was already there. You have any properties like that, Ms. Singer?"

"I'm sorry, I don't. At least, not at this moment. You never know when something might come on the market though. Farmers are having a hard go these days." It was heartbreaking to see that change so drastically since I had left town. "What kind of price are you thinking?"

He told me the figure and I clenched my jaw to keep it from dropping. He was crazy or had a vision of something that was headed off the charts.

"Well, maybe another realtor in the area will be able to help me." He masked his features, rolled up his drawings and slid them into the tubes they'd come out of.

"We all know each other's properties, Mr. Barnett. Realtors have a cooperative attitude in our county. If there was something like that represented by a different agency, I'd be aware of it." His raised an eyebrow and an almost-sneer showed he didn't believe me.

"I'll see what I can find. Thank you for your time." He reached to shake my hand and I gave him a business card.

"And I have your card too, Mr. Barnett." I stood it up in my computer keyboard so he'd see I had it quickly accessible. "If something comes on the market, I'll give you a call." I forced a smile, hoping I looked more confident—and less hungry for the commission—than I felt. "Perhaps we'll be speaking again soon."

After he left, I stood looking up at the county map framed on one wall. I wracked my brain to think where a parcel that large, in the type of location he'd described, might still exist. There just weren't any that I could think of, but I could ask somebody at the Standish farm if they had any suggestions. After all, I'd been gone a long time, and although I had seen much of the county since returning, I was still out of touch to some extent.

As I pulled into the parking area by Lillian's house, I noticed an unfamiliar car sitting there. I got out and went up onto the porch, and just when I would have knocked, the door swung open. Mathew flung himself against me, hugging my legs.

"Mommy! Hi, Mommy. Guess what we maked."

I crouched down to him and kissed the side of his chocolaty mouth.

"Um. Chocolate chip cookies?"

His eyes got round and he hugged me around the neck.

"Yes! Me and Miss Lillian maked 'em. You want one?"

"Goodness, yes I do. Miss Lillian is about the most famous chocolate chip cookie maker in the world."

Matthew rushed into the kitchen. Lillian had taught him how to carefully place a few cookies on a plate and serve them to a guest, complete with a napkin.

When I stood, I saw Lillian sitting on the couch beaming at Matthew's enthusiasm. A handsome man with sharp brown eyes sat next to her, but rose and walked toward me.

"Hello, Melissa." He held out his hand as if to shake mine, but I hugged him instead.

"David. It's been forever. I take it you've met my

son."

"Are you kidding? He and I basically solved all the world's problems at the kitchen table this afternoon." He turned to Matthew as he came back in, cautiously carrying a plate toward me. "Isn't that right, Matthew?"

Matthew nodded sagely. "I told Mr. David people need to be nice to each other and eat cookies." He handed me the plate and the napkin that had gotten a little creased in his hand, then beamed up at me.

"There you have it. Cookies save the world." David's smile was genuine and he patted Matthew on the shoulder gently. When he relaxed a little, I noticed that David's eyes looked tired.

"It's nice to see you. Are you home for the weekend?"

"Yes, just got here. And I imagine much of my weekend will be spent being bullied by my older brother. He's trying to turn me into a Christmas tree farmer, but I keep telling him my specialty is marketing." He shrugged, looking amused. "I try to stay with my strengths."

I chuckled. "He's difficult to deal with at times, I

suppose."

"You know better about that than many."

Though I didn't see any malice on his face, the comment stung. Old wounds were best left alone, if possible. Even though I'd been coming to the farm twice a day for a while now, I hadn't seen Jim since our first day back in town. He seemed to make an effort to stay out of my way, and that suited me fine.

At David's graceless remark, Francie kicked him in the ankle from her seat in an armchair where she continued to page through a magazine. He winced but only whispered the epithet that came to his lips. Of course, Francie was on my side. I would have expected as much, although so much time had passed, there shouldn't be a need for sides at all. What's a broken heart or two among friends?

"You're a realtor, Melissa. I keep telling Mom she should consider selling the farm and getting a nice little apartment in town," he said. "Let somebody else take the job of providing Christmas to the entire southern half of Indiana. What do you think?"

I could only stare at him.

"Uh. Melissa?" David waved a hand in front of my face.

"Oh. Oh, sorry. I was—I was thinking of…you know, work…stuff." I crossed my arms. "Sell? You want to sell the farm?"

"Oh, honey, no," Lillian insisted. "David is pulling your leg. And mine." She sent David a hard look. "This is the Standish Christmas Tree Farm, and that's what it'll be as long as I live. Harry wouldn't hold with me selling, for goodness' sake."

"Plus where would everybody move?" Francie tossed the magazine onto the coffee table. "The whole fam damily lives on the farm. David, you know it doesn't make sense."

"What doesn't make sense is for us to try to keep up this sham. None of us has the time for the farm. Much as we love Mom and loved Dad, this farm isn't the dream for us that it was for them."

Francie glared at him. "So you're ready to find a new place to live? Sell your lot and house and buy a condo in Louisville?"

David leaned against the door frame facing his

sister, his arms crossed. "I could."

"And Carla? I guess we just assume she wants out?"

"She has her shop. Plus Carla doesn't really need to be in Serendipity. She could do her business anywhere," David insisted. "Most of her big paying clients order on*line*, not on the Serendipity town square."

"Carla loves it here," I said softly.

"Of course she does." Lillian agreed.

David stepped back to the center of the room. "What about you, Francie? You own a two acre lot, same size as the rest of us, in your corner of the property. Yet you've lived away from here 'til—a few months ago. I don't see a house going up on that lot. What are your plans? Staying to help with Christmas, or ditching the small town life again, once Mom is okay to be on her own?"

"I am completely fine to be on my own," Lillian huffed.

"And then there's Jim."

I wasn't even sure who said it, because I was

watching Jim walk into the room. He must have come in through the back door and through the kitchen. His face was flushed and his green eyes flashed.

"Yeah, don't forget *old Jim*. What the *hell* kind of a fight is this to have in front of company?"

"She's not company." David took a step back. "This is Melissa, for God's sake. We've all been friends since elementary school. We have no secrets from her."

Jim reached his hand down and Matthew, tears streaming down his face, put his little hand into it. They walked together toward the kitchen, then Jim swung Matthew into his arms, and spoke over his shoulder to the rest of us.

"Matthew is our company, and he doesn't deserve to be in the middle of a bunch of grown-ups who can't mind their manners." He turned toward me. "Mel, I'm getting his jacket and taking him outside to say goodbye to Daisy. You want to meet us out there?"

I'm pretty sure I nodded yes.

Nobody said anything. The only sound in the house was Jim's boot treads across the vinyl kitchen floor and the back door closing softly.

Everyone in the living room looked at each other silently. I picked up Matthew's blanket from the child-size rocking chair he occupied to watch TV, and let myself out the front door. I gulped cool fresh air and calmed my nerves, then followed the sound of happy barking.

Jim and Matthew stood hand-in-hand watching Daisy retrieve a stick Jim had thrown. Matthew was smiling now. I crouched down in front of him.

"Hi, Sweetie. You okay?"

He nodded. "Yes. They were mad."

"Not mad, pardner. Just real tired, I think." Jim looked into the distance, not noticing us or Daisy who was ready to chase the stick again.

"Are you tired, Mr. Jim?"

He smiled down at the child. "Maybe a little. Christmas is coming though. There's lots to do. People need their trees." He looked at me and I saw for the first time the dark circles under his eyes. "It's what we do here. You know?"

I nodded, wiping a hot tear from the corner of my eye.

"Yes, I know. Your dad loved it, and didn't mind the work. You're all just trying to carry on the tradition."

Looks like it's quite a struggle.

"I don't have a dad," Matthew announced.

"I don't have one either, but I used to. He was a real nice man, Matthew. You would have liked him, and he would have loved having you around. He would love how you help Miss Lillian, and play with Daisy."

"Sometimes I can give Daisy a treat, if Miss Lillian says so."

"Yep. That's special stuff, Matthew. People who take good care of animals, and nature—those are special people. I always trust people like that the most."

"People who take care of children, and talk nicely to them, are pretty special too," I added, laying a hand on Jim's sleeve.

"Yeah, well." He looked down at my hand. "Anyway...I have lots of work to do. Looks like I'm not getting any help from David tonight."

"I'm so sorry about that."

Jim shrugged. "Not to worry. By tomorrow his

mood will have blown over. David comes home all tied up in knots. Usually overnight they straighten out and he's back to his usual self—almost bearable. I'll find some really fun projects for him tomorrow, I assure you. He likely doesn't realize how good the farm is for him, emotionally and physically. I don't mind telling you that, because there's no way anybody would believe it came out of my mouth."

Daisy wagged her tail and barked at Matthew, and he sped off with her to chase back and forth and throw the stick as far as his little arm could manage. It made me laugh to see how much fun he was having.

"This farm is a wonderful place. I'm grateful Matthew is able to spend some time here. I have such terrific memories from when I visited here as a kid."

"And older than a kid too, as I recall."

"Yes, well. A lot of that time you barely tolerated me." Would it be possible to keep things light with Jim, not dredge up the ugly part of our past?

"Not true. But as you grew up, I found you much easier to tolerate. Having you and Alice for friends was some pretty good thinking on the parts of my sisters."

"Then why did you give us such a hard time?"

"Because I liked you. Both you and Alice. But mainly you, Mel." He touched a finger to the little cleft in my chin, then slid his fingers through some of the hair that had come out of my headband. "I had an awful time trying to forget you after you left."

"I would have said you'd forgotten me *before* I left." And whose fault was it that he was trying to forget me at all? I was the innocent victim here.

He winced. "No. No. In fact I sure didn't. I said I tried."

"You managed to push the memory to the side then, when you married Diana."

He stiffened and dropped the lock of hair and slid his hands into his jacket pockets.

"I'd rather never hear that name again."

"That's funny. I feel the same way." I wanted to scream it at him. I'd wanted to scream at him for years about what he'd done, and there'd never been an opportunity. Now wasn't the time either—with my innocent son playing a few yards away, and the Standish family in the house.

He looked past me, a nerve twitching in his jaw.

"Mel, you have no idea what she did to me."

I took a deep breath. "I'm certain you deserved it to some extent. I'll leave it at that." If Diana treated him the way he had treated me, then I could almost applaud her efforts.

"Why did you leave the way you did?"

"My heart was broken, my self-esteem had gone from bad to non-existent, and the guy who dealt the final blow was the brother of my best friends. I couldn't stay in Serendipity and run into you every time I saw Francie or Carla. Or just run into you, because it's a small town and that's what happens." I shuddered, suddenly chilled. "We all went off to college. I just chose never to come back. Simple enough." Leaving and making my own life somewhere else had helped me heal—or I thought it had, until seeing Jim again.

"I'm amazed you stayed friends with Francie and Carla and Alice, if you hated Serendipity that much."

"I never hated Serendipity. It was boring to us when we were teenagers, but now I'm sure we all see the positives of small-town living. We were lucky to grow up here, weren't we?"

He nodded, not sure where I was going with this. Maybe not wanting to know, which made me want to lay it out for him.

"My family was so messed up. I can say that now, but at the time I wouldn't have wanted to admit it. I don't think anyone used the term 'dysfunctional' back then, but we were it. My brothers were much older, and idolized by Mom and Dad because they'd been these big sports heroes. Then I came along, the only girl, the only one in the family who loved books and learning. My parents fought each other my whole life, it seemed, and I was put in the middle of it. When they weren't fighting each other, my mother would start in on me. I was plain looking...no boy would ever love me...I'd never get married or have children."

Jim frowned and made a groaning sound. I was glad it bothered him to hear this.

I took a deep breath and looked over at the Standish home. "All I wanted at the time was to feel loved. Your family did that for me. Your mom and dad never minded when I'd come to spend the night, the weekend, or whatever. I was never made to feel as if I was in the way or a bother."

I shifted my gaze back to Jim. "Why my parents have stayed married I don't know. To this day, they still bicker constantly. I seldom take Matthew to visit, and to be honest, I don't think it matters to them. My brothers and their kids and current girlfriends are still the favorites. It's so wrong to raise kids that way, in competition with each other. Your family wasn't like that. Your family was about love and acceptance—and obviously still is. Matthew and I feel welcome here, and that is an amazing gift."

"Wow, Mel. I knew your parents were, you know, difficult, but you never went into it much. I'm surprised you didn't confide in me back when we were so close."

I shrugged. "They were my parents. What could anyone have done back then? What would you have done? One thing I know is that my chaotic upbringing made me stronger. I don't play doormat for anybody. That includes you, Jim Standish, no matter how nice you are to Matthew."

I blew out a breath that puffed in a white cloud. It

was cooling down quickly tonight. "I do thank you for your kindness to Matthew. You really have been good to him. Just—don't get the idea that I forgive you. That will never happen."

"So why come back to Serendipity now?"

"Kind of a strange series of occurrences. Life was going along fine, then all kinds of doors shut in my face. The one that was standing open with a big welcome mat was the Osborne house, which I've always wanted. You might say that's all coincidence, but I disagree. The most important thing is this is the right place to raise Matthew, and I know we'll have a good life."

"Why the Osborne place?"

"Living there, and holding my head up, is something I've wanted to do for a lot of years. You may or may not have a clue why that would be important to me."

He looked away from me, back into the distance. "Everybody has to deal with their past the best way they can. You've changed a lot, Mel, and all for the good. You were pretty in high school, but twenty years later, you're seriously beautiful. I can see you've been through some stuff and overcome it." He looked at me then, deeply into my eyes and I refused to flinch. "You're hiding something, though. Any chance you're going to tell me what it is?"

I shook my head. "None at all. Thanks again for watching out for Matthew." I called to him and he trotted over to me, happy and panting as much as the big black dog.

"I gotta go home now, Mr. Jim. See you tomorrow."

"That's a plan, pardner."

Daisy walked us to the SUV but Jim just stood there, the question still in his smile as he waved when I drove away. Was he bluffing about me hiding something?

Turning onto Tree Farm Road, I started a jazz CD to help calm me down. I checked the rearview and saw Matthew's smile hadn't dimmed a bit. He pulled a little plastic truck out of his backpack and ran it back and forth along the window ledge of the car.

What a day. A face-off among the members of the

Standish family about the future of the farm, an unpleasant stroll down memory lane with Jim, and Jared Barnett asking about a big rolling property with a lake and lots of trees.

I was either in the right place at the right time, or all heck was about to break loose.

CHAPTER SIX

The girls' day out we had started to plan all those weeks ago finally happened, in the form of an early Christmas shopping trip to Louisville. Francie and Carla assured me that Lillian would be hurt if she didn't get to watch Matthew while we were gone. I hadn't spoken to any of them about the blowup in the family living room that day, and I sure wouldn't say anything about the little talk Jim and I had afterward. If I was super lucky, I could drop Matthew off at the door as I did each weekday morning, and not see Jim at all. But 'super lucky' wasn't descriptive of my recent experiences. When I pulled up to Lillian's house and Matthew scrambled out of his car seat, he dashed straight toward Jim who was coming around the corner with Daisy at his heels.

"He sure likes Jim. But there's no accounting for taste." Carla stepped down off the front porch smiling, as Jim swung the little boy up in the air, resulting in squeals of delight.

Lillian came out then, wiping her hands on a kitchen towel. "You girls have fun now. We'll be just fine. I have plenty to keep these boys busy all day."

The identical look of mock horror on Jim and Matthew's faces was priceless, and chuckling, Lillian turned on her heel and went back into the house.

"I suppose it's natural for him to gravitate toward a male role model," I said, wanting to be realistic about it. "Just weird for Jim to fill that capacity, however temporarily."

"Not so weird, honey." Francie pulled out her cell phone and sent a text. "You're like family, so Jim is kind of a brother to you." She smiled innocently. "Right?"

"Right. That's it."

"I texted Alice that we're on our way, so let's get

moving." Francie slid the cell back into her bag. "That girl needs a day out more than the rest of us, I'd bet."

"I feel bad for being so caught up in my work I haven't gotten over to see Alice. Of course, I guess the street runs both ways."

"I don't see her much these days either," Carla said, opening the door of her Mustang and sliding in behind the wheel.

"Is she okay?" I asked.

"Sure. I think so. It's just, you know, I wish she'd done something more with her life. Instead of settling for Dean. Don't get me wrong." she hurried to say. "Dean is a very good guy. Alice chose him, so we have to be nice to him."

"I don't. I don't even live in Serendipity anymore." Francie's home was in Florida, but she had put her own life on hold to be with Lillian for a while after Harry's death.

"Could have fooled me, sister. You've been here how long?"

"A few months. I'm helping Mom."

"Sure." Carla slowed as a squirrel ran across the

road, hesitated, and headed back the same way he'd come. "Yes, you're helping Mom. But Mom's doing fine now, don't you think? I mean, considering... What's *really* going on with you, Francie? Is your marriage in trouble too?"

I felt way out of the loop. "What do you mean, 'too?' Alice's marriage is in trouble?"

"If it isn't, that's just because Alice has the patience of a saint. Or more likely, she's given up wanting more from life," said Carla.

"You're psychoanalyzing. Are dress designers supposed to psychoanalyze in their free time?" Francie was staring furiously at the back of Carla's head.

"Dress designers are just like bartenders. People tell us things. Not sure why a fitting room seems to turn into a confessional so often, but I've learned to just listen and make encouraging comments here and there. An awful lot of married women in this town seem unhappy, though I don't exactly keep count."

"You should publish your findings, Carla. I don't know what scientific journal would want to do that for you. Is *MAD Magazine* still out there?" Francie laughed at her own joke.

Carla stopped the powerful Mustang in front of a tidy white house on Walnut Street and blew the horn.

"Um. I don't mind going up and ringing the bell," I offered, opening the car door.

"Nah. She'll be ready. You will have to get out though, and let her in the back seat."

"Carla is having her second childhood. No boring four-door vehicles for her. Right, sis?"

Carla nodded, watching the house. "I'm usually by myself anyway, and heaven forbid somebody ask me to babysit and carry a child seat." She turned to me. "No offense. Matthew is terrific. I'm just not motherly, I guess. And after you hear about unhappy relationships all day long, it's easy to say I'm going to stay single and childless."

Francie sighed, looking out the side window. "You might change your mind, if the right man came along."

"Breaking up a relationship is rough—I should know. But I'm sure glad I never ended up with a child to raise alone." She hit the steering wheel with one hand. "Melissa, I'm sorry. I keep saying the wrong things here. You ladies might have to carry the conversation without me, if I can't do any better than this. I'll have you all hating me in no time."

"I don't listen to you anyway, sweetie," Francie smiled at her sister and batted her eyelashes.

"Hey, don't worry about hurting my feelings, Carla," I said. "Because I—"

Alice appeared and waved at us, turned to be sure her front screen door shut securely, and then smiled toward the Mustang. I climbed out of the car and hugged her.

"Hey, girlfriend. I'm so glad you could make it. We've got loads of time to catch up on anything and everything." I squeezed Alice's hands. "Uh—front or back seat? It's been pointed out that we're living Carla's second childhood, if you didn't know."

Carla waved a diamond-draped hand. "Hey, the way I look at it, this is the vixenmobile, ladies. You haven't lived until you've driven down the street of anywhere but Serendipity, with the top down on this gorgeous car. Right, Alice?"

"Right." Alice took sunglasses out of her handbag

and slid them on her nose. "Beautiful women stylin' in our big, dark shades, music turned up. There's always plenty of attention from the guys." She giggled and suddenly looked years younger.

"Yep. And the stink eye from the women *with* those guys." Carla pulled a bright silk scarf out of her bag and tied it around her thick dark hair.

"Sounds to me like you two are troublemakers," said Francie, leaning against her headrest. She cleared her throat. "So. Can you put the top down, Carla?"

"Yeah, Carla," I chimed in while wondering if we'd all end up with pneumonia. "Francie and I want the full experience."

"You sure you're up for that? I don't mind—as long as it's not raining, I'm happier with it down all year. I just crank up the heat or A/C." She pulled to a stop in a parking lot, flipped the levers to release the top, and pushed the button to retract it. A minute later we were sailing down State Road 135 with the radio blasting hits from the 1970s. The heater blew full-force.

"She's my own sister and never took me for a ride like this before," Francie shouted a while later over the wind, music, and road noise.

"You've been staying pretty close to Mom since you came home," yelled back Carla.

"A little break once in a while...would be nice." Francie finished the sentence a little softer. I looked back at Francie and wondered if she was sorry she'd said it at all.

We rode for a while without talking much but sang along with the radio when we knew the words. Carla beat on the steering wheel for percussion on her favorite songs. I felt young and free, and didn't care that the wind was tying my long hair into knots.

By the time we got to the next little town, a cold mist had begun. Carla pulled over in the empty lot of a nearby bank and put the top back up.

"Hate to do this, ladies."

I wanted to say something encouraging but was pretty sure my teeth would chatter too loudly. Half an hour later, we were in a Louisville shopping mall, drinking designer coffee and trying to form our strategy.

"I need to hit the big stores," Carla said. "I've

made Mom's gift—a fabulous bathrobe, and…really all I need is stuff for Jim and David—and Matthew. Ooh, I need help with that, Mel. I bought gift cards for my employees, though I don't like the impersonal way that feels. It's what they'll enjoy though." She shrugged. "What about you ladies?"

I was pretty sure that hesitation meant she was making things for the rest of us too. I hoped so because Carla's work was gorgeous. We decided to split into pairs for the rest of the morning, meet for lunch, and then mix up the pairs for the afternoon. That way I could shop for Francie whenever I wasn't shopping *with* Francie, for example.

"Last thing, we'll all hit the toy store together and get stuff for Matthew, okay?" Francie pulled a list out of her jeans pocket. "At the toy store, I'm shopping on Mom's behalf too. She wants to buy him a toy farm." She looked up at me. "She wants your okay on it, Mel. The rest of her shopping she's done online."

We met at one of the mall restaurants for lunch. Everybody had several pretty bags of secrets, which we would divvy up in portions of the trunk before heading out again after we ate.

"What about the Christmas shop?" I asked. "Are you guys doing that this year?"

Francie stirred her hot tea. "Christmas shop is covered. Mom and I did an inventory and she knew the companies she orders from. We ordered it all online, and stuff should arrive in time to open."

"That's a relief," said Alice. "I wasn't sure she'd have the heart to even deal with it."

"She forced herself, as you can imagine," said Francie. "She feels so strongly that she owes it to Dad to make sure the farm keeps going."

"She can't do that on her own, of course. After that day when David suggested you sell, has that been discussed anymore?" I wanted to know and didn't want to know at the same time. What kind of friend would I be to let them sell for less than it was worth? And what kind of friend would I be to push them toward selling, if they weren't ready?

"Mom is adamant that the farm keeps going," said Francie, and Carla nodded. "Unfortunately, the bulk of the work falls to Jim because he makes himself available for it. I did a little tree trimming with him this summer, but he did most of it, and that's after working all day."

"Not like he's digging ditches all day, Francie," said Carla. "He sits in a chair and pushes papers."

"And occasionally makes a trip to the courthouse. But the stress of being a lawyer, you know. Mom worries about Jim's health. She's afraid he'll have a heart attack like Dad."

"And die out among the trees, with none of us there to help him." Carla fiddled with her salad, not eating. "You just can't help wondering what would have happened if one of us had been there when Dad.... Mom blames herself—I know she does."

"But that's the way your dad was, right?" Alice touched Francie's hand and Carla's. "He loved being out there among the trees, working. He was so happy doing that. Maybe it's the way he would have wanted to die."

"He would have hated getting feeble and having to depend on Mom or one of us to do things for him. That's for sure." Francie wiped a tear and took a sip of tea.

"And he wasn't alone when he died. That's one thing. Daisy was with him." I re-stated this because the girls had told me about it soon after their dad's death. "I'm sure that was a comfort to him. Don't you think?"

Francie and Carla nodded.

"Daisy's whole life, wherever Dad went, she was with him, or at least tried to go. Jim said that when he found Dad…Daisy was right there with him, laying so still he thought maybe she was dead too."

The grieving Daisy had whimpered for days, and it had been weeks before her appetite returned. Now Daisy was running and playing again with Matthew.

"It's so much fun to see Daisy and Matthew together." Francie said. "Mom and I love watching them in the back yard through the kitchen window. I haven't seen Daisy have that much energy…." She let the sentence trail off. "Mom says Matthew makes her feel alive again. You can see he does that for Daisy too. It's great how they fit together."

We were silent for a few minutes, in our own thoughts.

"So what's the right answer for your family? About the farm," asked Alice, looking from Francie to Carla.

"Dunno. This year it's Christmas as usual—as much as we can manage without Dad, anyway. We've been working in that direction, but I dread opening day like crazy," Carla said.

Francie nodded. "I do too, and I don't even know what to expect after being gone so long. Brad always wanted us to have Christmas in our own home, and come here for New Year's."

"Car loads of people pulling up for about a month straight, looking for the perfect Christmas tree procurement experience," said Carla. "Complete with Mannheim Steamroller on the loudspeaker inside and outside the shop, hand-saws loaned to them so they can wander the acres of trees to find the perfect one. Then, when they find it, they drag it back and one of us helps tie it to the top of their vehicle. SUVs are the worst. Have to get the step-ladder. While we're doing that, maybe the mom or kids wander into the shop and find ornaments or cookies or candy or wassail mix or big angels to set on the mantel. You know, whatever will make their home perfect for the holidays."

Alice put an arm around Carla. "I'm sorry. I know it's going to be so hard. Your dad always was laughing and whistling when Dean and I came out to get our tree. And back when I was a kid and went with Mother and Dad, I remember how much fun he made it for everyone. I thought then Mr. Standish was one of Santa's special helpers." She shook her head. "Maybe my mom said that, but I do remember thinking it."

Carla and Francie were beaming at the memory of their dad, but at the edge of tears.

"Maybe I can help some if you need me," I offered. "Not sure how Matthew could fit into that. Maybe I can find a sitter." I hated the idea of leaving him, since evenings and weekends were our time together.

"Me too," said Alice. "And Dean would be glad to help, I'm sure. He'd be good at tying trees onto people's cars, sharpening the saws, and things like that. He knows the different kinds of trees too, so he could help people with information."

"Funny thing," said Carla. "You might think bad weather would cut down on crowds, but if it snows, we have a deluge of customers. They think they're going to have a Norman Rockwell moment."

"Or Currier and Ives."

"Or *Christmas Vacation.* It's usually a combination," Carla said, chuckling. "This year you know what I'll miss?"

She looked at each of us in turn. "*I'll be Home for Christmas.*"

Francie groaned, grinning. "Dad whistled that song all the time. I'd forgotten."

"Yes you've been gone a few years. Dad whistled *I'll be Home for Christmas* nearly constantly from Thanksgiving to Christmas Day. I remember when I was maybe twenty, asking him to pick another song. He just smiled and kept on whistling. It drove me nuts."

"David tried wearing ear plugs one year but he couldn't hear the customers talking, so Dad made him take them out." Francie giggled.

"I'm sure that song has been on the radio a few thousand times already." Carla looked down into her mug. "Christmas music starts in October anymore. I haven't heard it yet, but I know I'll cry when I do."

"No doubt." Alice patted her hand.

"Poor Mom. I don't know how she manages." Francie shook her head. "You know? When it's this hard on us, you know it's horrible for her."

"They were such a couple. Did everything together. They both loved the holidays so much and were the first in our area to have a Christmas tree farm. I understand her wanting to keep the farm going because of that." Carla drained her mug and set it down carefully.

So we'd returned to the original topic and of course nothing had changed. There didn't seem to be a good solution, and Christmas season was nearly upon us.

CHAPTER SEVEN

The Sunday before Thanksgiving, I took Matthew for the first time to the church I attended as a child. Some people remembered me, but everyone was charmed by Matthew. After the service, as we filed out the minister solemnly shook Matthew's hand.

"I'm glad to meet you, Matthew. You be sure and come back next week because we'll have a big Christmas tree in the sanctuary. The children get to help decorate it. Won't that be fun?"

"Sure. Are you getting your Christmas tree from Mr. Jim? He has the best ones."

The minister laughed. "Well, we certainly are. We always get a Standish tree."

"That's good. I work there," said Matthew, puffing up importantly.

"Really?"

"Yes. I help Mr. Jim with the trees. Sometimes we ride the four-wheeler to the back forty." He looked down, concentrating hard to get the two halves of the zipper on his jacket lined up. "And I help Miss Lillian in the Christmas shop." The zipper went up smoothly and Matthew beamed into the minister's eyes. "Christmas is coming."

"So it is," the minister chuckled. Patting Matthew's shoulder gently, he then stood up to face me. "Sounds like the Standish family has some especially good help this year."

****

Matthew was keyed up by the conversation and barely ate any lunch. "Mommy, can we go to the farm? I might need to work today."

"Sweetie, they may not be working since it's Sunday."

"Please? Can you call? I miss it when I go to school."

Although Lillian had insisted she loved having Matthew and he was no trouble at all, we all realized she and Francie needed to spend time getting the Christmas shop ready for the season, so I had decided to find a preschool for Matthew. It was one thing to order the stock and put it on the shelves, but Francie and Carla said their mother had decided to overhaul the whole place this year. She planned to take all the shelving and tables out, give the place a fresh coat of glossy snow-white paint, then paint the fixtures, and put them back in. And *then* put all the merchandise on display. With Matthew to care for every day, that chore would have been impossible.

It had been late in the semester, but with some cajoling, I had been able to get Matthew into a preschool three days a week. This had been Matthew's first week of school, and he had enjoyed it but missed his friends at the farm. So, without giving it another thought, I gave in.

I sent a text to Francie, and she replied they'd love

for us to come out. As usual anymore, Jim was right there when we arrived. Daisy trotted along with him as he got off the four-wheeler and approached Lillian's house. Matthew ran over to them and Jim swung him up into the air.

Once he was back on the ground, Matthew asked, "Mr. Jim, can Daisy and me ride on your four-wheeler? Please."

Jim looked at me. "Mel, how do you ever look down into those eyes and say no?"

Jim and Matthew sent identical, quizzical expressions my way.

"It's not easy. But you can't say 'yes' when the right answer is 'no.' Just because it's easier to go along with whatever the request is, doesn't mean you should do it." I sighed. "Sometimes it's just being the bad guy. I feel that way a lot."

Jim smiled and shook his head. "You're not a very believable bad guy." He crouched down to Matthew's eye level. "Sorry, pardner. We could maybe all go in my truck though."

"Yay! Miss Lillian too?"

"Sure, if she wants to. How about you ask her?"

"Okay!" Matthew raced to the house, knocked loudly a couple of times, and burst in. As part of the family now, he knew the routine. Jim walked toward me, Daisy milling around him, as if she knew a truck ride was in her future.

"Mel, you up for a tour?"

"Oh. Well, we came out to see if you needed help."

"I get that. We can always use Matthew's help. He's everybody's bright spot these days. It'd be nice for you to see more of the farm. We'll have plenty of chaperones, so it should be safe."

Safe for me—or for you, Jim?

Lillian came out the front door, pulling on her jacket as Matthew chattered encouragement. She was smiling and had a nice pink color in her cheeks. Yep, Matthew's enthusiasm had done a lot of good for Lillian, it seemed.

"This is a fun surprise on a Sunday afternoon." She hugged me, then turned to Jim. "I hear we're taking a drive, son. Matthew seems to think the three of us are going to sit in the cab with Daisy on our laps." She reached down and touched the boy's head. "But my guess is that Daisy will be in the bed. How do you see it working?"

"In the bed? Not the truck?" Matthew looked back and forth from Lillian to Jim.

"The back of the truck is called the bed, pardner." Jim let down the tailgate and Daisy immediately jumped in and ran toward the cab end. He closed the tailgate again with a slam. "There. Now she has plenty of room. Once we get going you'll see how she rides. Then I bet you'll be glad Daisy's not up front with us." He opened the passenger door and looking at me, raised one eyebrow. "Coming with us, Mel?"

"Mommy! Yes, you ride too."

Jim helped Mathew up into the cab, and then gave his mom a hand up too. Then it was my turn. I squeezed in and turned to pull the door closed, but Jim was still standing there.

Just looking in my eyes and smiling. I had no idea how long that lasted. A few seconds or a couple of minutes—no idea. Nothing else seemed to exist.

"Hey! We're burnin' daylight."

We all laughed at Matthew's cowboyism. Jim winked at me and pushed the door gently closed. Lillian was whispering something to Matthew, so maybe that wink was our secret. It was a tiny delight to have that one sweet moment between the two of us, without any snide comment alongside it.

So long ago there had been many little moments like that—a secret smile, a wink no one else saw. Shared dreams. It had been a long time since anything positive had existed between us.

****

In preparation for our senior prom night, some of the moms got together and organized a party for afterward. Back then the junior class had the job of decorating the gymnasium, and only juniors and seniors could attend the dance. This year's junior class had done an outstanding job of transforming the place into a tropical paradise. Grass huts, a semi-believable waterfall, and big colorful raffia flowers everywhere. To go along with the theme, these moms had convinced

Mr. and Mrs. Osborne to host an after-prom party for a bunch of us kids. There were some other after-prom parties at houses in town too, and a lot of kids went to restaurants in Louisville afterward instead, which was way cooler, but parents didn't like it because of the distance and safety concerns. But I wasn't one of the cool kids, just brainy. Jim was smart and handsome and very cool, partly because he was quarterback of the football team. But since Lillian was one of the organizers, and she and Harry were good friends of the hosts, he was pretty much forced into the event at the Osborne house.

Jim and I were an item, and had been our whole senior year. Alice Campbell was in our class and was going to prom with Dean Campbell after a brutal breakup from hunky Jamison Kincaid. Jim and I were in the prom king and queen competition. Fortunately, the couple that won actually ended up getting married and still are as far as I know. It would have been awful to look at yearbooks down the road and be faced with yourself and Mr. Wrong, wearing matching Prom Royalty crowns. Jim's sister Carla was a junior, David a sophomore, and Francie was a freshman.

The Osbornes were a really nice, middle-aged couple. Their kids were older than us, out of college, and living their lives someplace interesting. Jim and I, and Carla and her date, whose name I've forgotten, drove the few blocks from the high school to the Osborne house and arrived a little after some of the others. I was surprised to see Diana Reynolds there. Sure, she was a senior too, but the crowd she usually ran with had ditched the end of prom and headed for Louisville. Diana's date was also a member of the football team. Greg was known as being a hard-hitter, and though he didn't always abide by the rules, he consistently got results the coach wanted. I didn't like or trust him and felt the same about Diana. I'm afraid it probably showed on my face or in my demeanor. There were thirty or so of us kids, playing music too loudly, eating lots of junk food, and swimming in the beautiful heated pool. At that time, there wasn't a pool house, so you had to change in a little bathroom just off the kitchen.

When Diana emerged in her bathing suit, it was as

if angels started singing and playing harps while aiming a spotlight at her. Anyway, that's the way Jim acted. He followed her and that barely-there bikini the rest of the night. It was disgusting. I was beyond angry, and Lillian and Carla took up for me with Jim. And if you know anything about teenage boys, you know that pressure from his mother and sister did nothing for me and everything to ruin the evening more thoroughly.

Well, Diana and her date headed for his car about the same time the four of us started out. Diana was still in the bikini, which clung damply to her, but had put her high heels back on and draped the shawl from her prom dress provocatively over one shoulder. Who knows where the rest of the dress had ended up. With that going on just a car length away, it's a wonder Jim was even able to remember how to get his car started.

He managed to drive me home, and left me on the doorstep with a peck on my cheek. I felt like slapping him, but Carla and what's-his-name were in the car watching. Prom was on a Friday or Saturday, and I didn't hear from Jim the rest of the weekend. On Monday at school everybody was talking about what had happened at the Osborne's party. Not just those of us who were there or even those who'd been at prom, but every single occupant of the entire school building was talking about the awful way Jim had treated me and salivated after Diana. I heard whispers all day long that Jim was getting ready to break up with me. By the end of the school day, I was nearly in tears, and whom did I meet in the hall near the art room door? Oh yeah, Ms. Bikini.

She just leered at me and said, "I guess you know he's mine."

Yes it was childish, and yes, if the relationship had been important to Jim and me, nothing would have come of any of it. But he called me that night and broke up with me. On the phone.

Pretty lame, huh?

Diana's dad was the circuit court judge. He had been a friend of Harry Standish for years, and they'd been on the football team together back in the stone ages. Jim had told everyone all through high school that he wanted to be a lawyer, and it worked out that way. Jim and Diana got married, her dad was a mentor to

Jim, and when he graduated and passed the bar, he got a job at the law firm Judge Reynolds had helped establish before running for judge.

It was all very cozy and happy.

And that Monday after prom, I could see the handwriting on the wall. I wasn't going to stay in Serendipity or come back after college and have to witness any more antics from Jim and Diana "Bikini" Standish. I was going to make my own life.

****

Jim started the truck and Daisy began running from side to side, barking joyfully.

"Boy, is she happy." said Matthew, twisting around to see.

"Yep. I don't take her along very often."

"She likes to go, Mr. Jim."

"Sure. But Daisy is Miss Lillian's dog. She stays there most of the time."

"Daisy is a good dog. Does she take care of you, Miss Lillian?"

"Yes, she does." Lillian sighed and looked out the windshield. "Pretty much everybody takes care of me these days."

"That's 'cause we love you," said Matthew, patting her hand.

Lillian turned back and kissed Matthew's cheek. She looked near tears.

"And 'cause you make great cookies. Right, Mr. Jim?"

"I couldn't agree with you more, pardner. On both counts." He smiled at his mom and she wiped a tear away, smiling too.

"I haven't been out this way in too long. Jim, you've kept everything looking wonderful. These trees are shaped just right."

"I haven't done it alone, of course."

She shook her head. "Most everything has fallen to you, honey, and I appreciate all you've done. Your father would be so proud." Maybe she'd been about to say more, but her voice broke, and we just rode along the track in companionable silence, except for Daisy's happy barks and the complaining truck springs when they hit the deeper ruts.

"What do you do to the trees, Mr. Jim?"

"Oh. Jim, honey, can you show him?"

"Sure." He stopped the truck and took a pair of pruners out of the big plastic toolbox in the bed. Daisy sat down, wagging her tail, likely wondering if the ride was over already. Jim let the tailgate down in case she wanted to run around, and then the rest of us piled out and followed him to a huge tree.

"This blue spruce is just going to grow and grow. We let some of them do that because it's so pretty. But to take home, people need trees that are smaller than that. And they want them to be shaped a certain way." He led us a few yards further. "Now, this tree is about your age, Matthew.

"Looky at this tree, Mommy! It's four like me!"

"Yes, I see."

Jim led us to a white pine, which had always been my favorite because of the soft needles.

"This one is growing really well, but when they're smaller I have to cut some out of the top so the tree grows fatter instead of growing up real skinny. Most people don't like skinny Christmas trees." He gestured with the pruners to a cut he'd made that summer. "See this? It's healed over, but that's where I had to trim this branch a little bit, to improve the shape of the tree."

Matthew examined the tip of the branch, touching it with one finger, and then ran his little hand along the needles. "It's soft. And it smells good." He took a deep breath and then stood silent for a bit, seeming to listen. "The trees are singing."

A strong breeze had begun to blow through the trees, creating a soughing sound. Lillian and Jim and I exchanged knowing smiles.

"That song is pretty," he said, looking at me for confirmation. I nodded. "This is the beautifullest farm, huh Mommy?"

Lillian gestured to the vista below us. "You just wait 'til there's snow on these trees, Matthew. And when people start coming here for their Christmas trees. That's when it's the very most beautiful."

"Christmas is fun!" Matthew was animated again, and grasped Lillian's hand. "You like Christmas, Miss Lillian?"

"Yes, I do. I love it. My husband loved it too. Jim and Carla and Francie and David's dad, he was my husband. And he loved Christmas more than anyone I've ever known. He worked hard all year so people could have the prettiest trees. And when it was almost Christmas time, he worked even harder, but the whole time he was smiling and happy because it's what he loved to do." She sighed.

"Now Mr. Jim does that?"

"A lot of it. But he has another job too, so it's hard on him."

"Oh, Mom."

"Well, it is. I don't want you having a heart attack and dying like your father, Jim."

"Mom, I'm perfectly fine. And besides I'm twenty years younger."

Matthew had been listening intently. "Mr. Jim needs a helper. He needs elves, like Santa."

"What a wonderful idea," Lillian said, smoothing Matthew's dark hair. I wonder where we could find some good elves."

"I don't know. This town maybe doesn't have

elves."

Lillian was thinking about something. "Maybe it does and we just didn't realize." She started toward the truck. "Everyone ready to head back? I think I need to make a few calls."

I was surprised at her change in attitude and wondered what she had in mind.

"O-kay. We're gonna call elves." Matthew hurried to catch up with Lillian.

Once again Jim and I had a moment, just a single moment, together.

"I don't know what she has in mind, but I like the light in her eyes." He turned his back to his mother and my son, blocking them from my view and me from theirs. "I'd like to see a light in your eyes too, Mel. Not only the kind you have when you're proud of your little boy, but the kind you used to have when you looked at me. I want you to know I'm making that a goal this Christmas season." He touched a finger to the little cleft in my chin, spun back around, and walked to the truck.

I followed a few paces behind, watched him put his pruners away. He called for Daisy and she ran out of the trees, happy and out of breath. Once she had jumped back up into the truck bed, Jim closed the tailgate again.

I watched it all with detachment, as if I weren't one of the people in this scene. After all, I had left this simple life behind years ago. So many times, I had been out on this farm with Carla and Francie, or with Jim, and seen the same landscape, felt the same breezes, smelled the fresh pine smell. It had been my second home back then, and yet not mine at all. Like now, when I cared about what happened here, but it really didn't have anything to do with me.

Why was I forever on the sidelines, wanting to be a part but not belonging?

The Standish farm had always been a peaceful oasis for me. As a kid I had run through the rows of trees playing hide and seek with the girls, and sometimes with David and Jim as well. When we were teenagers, Alice, Carla, Francie and I had many important discussions in the cool, quiet privacy of the evergreens. When Jim and I were dating, there were secluded places on the farm where he could drive his car and not be seen. We lay on an old blanket spread over the car hood and watched shooting stars that were brighter here than anywhere else. We talked about the future, and, of course, we made out. But Jim hadn't pushed me further. He respected and cared for me—I had thought.

My own family lived in a crowded neighborhood of small clapboard houses in a grimy part of Serendipity. There was never enough room or enough privacy, and in the summer there didn't even seem to be enough air to breathe in our part of town. Shortly after I graduated from SHS, the biggest factory in town closed, and my parents moved to the Indianapolis area where my dad and mom both found jobs. There would never be a reason for them to move back to this little town.

I still had moments of second guessing my own decision to return.

Part of it was business. I knew I could take up the slack left by the retiring Parkers. My name was local, which means a lot in a small town, and although it wasn't famous, at least it didn't have any black marks by it. The second reason was that Serendipity, though not perfect, was a better place for me to raise Matthew.

Alice and the Standish family were like family to me, and were becoming that way for Matthew. I wouldn't have had a head start on a career anywhere like I did here, and the difference in cost of living between a large city and Serendipity was major.

The last reason was the house. Which of course was how the conversation began in the first place. But if the rest of the factors hadn't been there, the Osborne house would have remained an unfulfilled dream.

The presence of Jim Standish in the midst of all this good karma was a bit confusing to my system. I didn't want to be around the guy who had dumped me for no reason. But since coming back to town, I hadn't seen any sign of that Jekyll/Hyde personality. I had only seen the Jim Standish who was a good son and brother, worked hard without complaint, and paid wonderful attention to Matthew. This is a man I really liked. I just had to remember—and remind him if necessary—that our relationship stopped at friendship, period.

Back at the house, Lillian invited us in for sugar cookies and hot cocoa. Matthew and I accepted, but Jim excused himself. He had convinced David to help him sharpen hand saws and get some other preparations made for the season.

"I guess you realize this Thursday is Thanksgiving." He looked as if he were gauging his mother's reaction, looking for signs of distress.

"Yes, son. That's why I bought a twenty-two pound turkey last week."

He shifted from one foot to the other. "First customers will show up."

She sighed. "Yes. I imagine I could name some who are always here the first day. I have calls to make this afternoon. My last orders for the Christmas shop are supposed to arrive tomorrow or Tuesday. Francie and Carla and I have accomplished great things in there, you know. We're nearly ready for the season to start."

"Okay. That's good, Mom."

"We'll make it, honey." Lillian put her hand in his and then grabbed mine too. "It's so very hard this year, but this is what we do."

Later, over cookies and hot cocoa, she told Matthew and me some of what they had accomplished this week. She was happy to have made so much progress, while dreading the heartache that she knew would accompany the holiday.

"Harry was everywhere during the season, you know," Lillian said wistfully, tracing with one finger the pattern of holly on her big white mug. "He handed out handsaws and showed people on the big map where to find the kinds of trees they wanted. He would turn up when someone had trouble cutting their tree and cut it down for them without making the person feel too embarrassed. He tied the trees to cars, dashed into the Christmas shop to get a cup of cocoa or wassail, and give me a kiss." She blushed. "Then he was gone again on some other errand. Always happy, always whistling his favorite Christmas song. My goodness, how we grew weary of that song, and yet—you know, it's just what we all need to hear now. Of course, I can't bear the thought of hearing it on the radio. I've made David promise to make a CD of Christmas music to play in the shop. Every single Christmas song there is *except that one*. Maybe next year, you know? Next year should be easier."

"You'll always miss him, Lillian. I hope nobody is trying to push you into 'getting over it,' because that's just wrong."

"Maybe a couple of people, friends of mine, think I should hurry up and get my grieving done. Those ladies are well-intentioned and loving, but they aren't widows. They don't understand what it is."

Heartbreaking. That's what it was to watch this woman who was missing the man who'd been her best friend for so many years. I couldn't imagine what it was like to live it first-hand.

She shook off the reverie and smiled gently. "I certainly hope we can plan on the two of you being here for lunch on Thanksgiving Day."

"Well—"

"We eat at noon, sharp. Everything has to be eaten, cleaned up, and leftovers put away because our first customers will arrive an hour before the posted opening time. I don't know why they can't wait one hour. I guess everybody has their traditions."

The farm was open to customers every weekday evening until Christmas Eve, and opened at noon on

Saturdays and Sundays. A grueling schedule I knew I would dread if it were my own, even without the lurking sadness of Harry's absence.

"Mommy? Please?"

Thanksgiving? It was a family event, and we weren't family. My parents had invited us to be with them for an early evening meal, but I wasn't looking forward to the round-trip drive knowing I needed to have my office open Friday as usual. You could never predict when someone would want to look at real estate, and as a new business owner, I needed to be known for excellent service.

"Lillian, I was just planning a little Thanksgiving feast for the two of us, followed by a viewing of the original *Miracle on 34th Street*. You know, just keep it low-key."

"Mommy! It's time to sell Christmas trees. I gotta work. Remember?"

Lillian smiled at me and I rolled my eyes, giving in without a fight. Who would want to crush a Christmas spirit like that?

"Okay if I bring Waldorf salad?"

"Perfect."

CHAPTER EIGHT

On Monday morning when I pulled into my driveway a little after eight, Jared Barnett was leaning on my doorbell. Matthew had been draggy this morning, so I was a few minutes late getting him to preschool and then driving back here. The sign on my door said the office opened at eight, and I adhere to that. Except for this one time, and you'd know it would happen with a potential client I wasn't sure what to do with. I parked the SUV in my drive instead of pulling all the way into the garage, then walked up onto the front porch where he stood.

"Mr. Barnett. Nice to see you again." I unlocked the door and opened it, preceding him into the spacious living area. It hit me every time I came in the front door, how open and almost empty this space was. It made me feel peaceful, not hemmed in.

Barnett was muttering something about the greasy breakfast and fuel-oil-flavored coffee he'd had at The Diner before coming here. Obviously, the man wasn't used to small towns. For all he knew, I was related to the owners of the diner. You just don't go around slinging words like that, unless you're prepared to have them slung back at you sometime.

I walked quickly behind my desk, gesturing for him to have a seat. "What can I do for you today?"

I saw his mental dismissal of something crude he'd like to have said. I silently counted to ten, trying not to dislike him or have any personal feeling about him at all. The guy was a potential business associate. Could be nothing, could be important—for me and for the Standish family, if they decided to go that way.

"Ms. Singer, you remember when I was here last and told you the type of property I'm looking for?"

"Yes, of course I do." I picked up a pen and slid a pad closer in case he was going to say something worth writing down. "Nothing has really changed on that though. No big parcels have come onto the market."

He leaned back and steepled his fingers. "No? Well, I think there's one you may have failed to mention. The Standish farm." His over-bright eyes bored into mine, watching for a reaction.

"To my knowledge, that farm isn't for sale." My voice was clipped. "I don't know where you heard otherwise."

He didn't move, barely blinked, keeping eye contact. Hoping I would flinch first?

"I realize it isn't exactly on the market, but I also know there are issues with the family. With the old man dead and his widow grief-struck, they're struggling to go on with business as usual." He sat up a bit straighter. "But it isn't business as usual, is it?" He shook his head, feigning concern for the afflicted family members.

"I understand what grief is, Ms. Singer. I've had my share." He sighed heavily. "It's difficult to decide it's time to let go of the past. But the Standish family needs to consider the present as well, and the future."

I wanted to interrupt him—shut him up—but found myself speechless as he continued his soliloquy.

"What of Jim and Carla and David? Do any of them have a chance to have normal lives when they're burdened by a tree farm as well as their own careers? And Francie, who's been here for months looking after her mother. Her husband must wonder when she'll come back to him. What kind of strife must this be inflicting on her marriage?

"Ms. Singer, I understand you know the Standish family quite well. And that your son is out there several days a week when he isn't at preschool. You care about them, I'm sure. Think about what all of this is doing to their health." He raised a hand. "I understand they're all relatively young. Except Lillian, of course. Wouldn't it make the best sense for the farm to sell, Lillian buy a nice little place in town where she can grow her flowers and get together with friends? Wouldn't it be better if Francie could go home, and come to visit when she wanted? Wouldn't David be better off in the city where he belongs? And Carla would have all the time she wanted to pursue her design career instead of putting it on hold because of the extra work she has to do. She'd have more time to spend with friends too, wouldn't she? And Jim. You know Jim has worked himself to exhaustion. What if he has a massive heart attack like his dad, out in the midst of those trees some evening? Who would know until it was too late? He doesn't have anybody—does he?" He raised a brow.

Barnett stood up and leaned both hands on my desk pleadingly. "Think about *them*, Ms. Singer. They deserve to be guided by someone with knowledge of the business, knowledge of their needs—and knowledge of the potential price for their property *at this moment in time*. Serendipity is close enough to Louisville to make this development successful. And you, Ms. Singer, are close enough to the Standish family to make the development happen in the first place. I think if you listen to your heart, you'll discover this is the right thing to do. Likely it's why you were led back to Serendipity in the first place. To broker this deal for the Standish family…and then see what results from it, for you and little Matthew. Your lovely home here is a demonstration of the fact that you appreciate the finer things in life. You and I both have an idea what your commission will be on the sale. It would do a lot for a college fund for the little guy."

Straightening again he smiled and extended his hand. "You think about that, please. I have confidence you'll do the right thing."

****

I locked the door briskly after Jared Barnett left, stood back a little and watched through the sheer curtain as he pulled away from the curb in that sleek BMW. The man was an incredible salesman—I had realized that the first time we met, but today I felt as if he'd reached into my soul and used its contents against me. Of course, I was already worried about the whole Standish family and what they were going through. I didn't need to have a total stranger point those things out to me.

Mr. Barnett had evidently found some chatty folks in town to be able to glean that much information about the Standish family, and about me. Not that it's difficult to find someone around here willing to share like that, but still somehow it was disconcerting to have it all thrown in my face at once. After a few minutes, I got a handle on my emotions and unlocked the door. It was office hours, for goodness sake—I couldn't very well leave the door locked.

Same with the situation at the farm. That wasn't something that could be locked away and ignored. It wasn't my place to solve the problems there, but I wanted to help. It was the least I could do as a friend. A potential commission wasn't the issue at all. So it would have been vastly easier to know I was considering presenting Mr. Barnett's idea to the Standishes because I cared about them, as opposed to foreseeing a huge improvement in my own bank account.

I was sure surprised to see the name and number of the local bed and breakfast show up on my phone when it began to trill. Mrs. Jenson, the proprietress, was concerned that one of her boarders was in Serendipity for nefarious reasons—possibly aimed at me. He had asked a lot of questions and had been pumping people for information. Seems he had been particularly inquisitive this morning when he'd had breakfast at The Diner. Mrs. Jenson's sister and brother-in-law own The Diner, and although they'd been happy enough to talk to the guy at first, when Barnett left, everybody in The Diner started wondering out loud about his purpose in Serendipity. One of the other customers said he had heard the guy asking nosy questions along the same line when he was having dinner at Al's Place the night before.

It was Mrs. Jenson's considered opinion that the people of Serendipity needed to stand up to anyone who would put their own interests before the interests of others. Especially when those people weren't "from here." And most especially, if they had an inclination to destroy a local landmark like the Standish Christmas Tree Farm.

Mrs. Jenson said her great-niece had gotten a call from Lillian Standish about working part time in the Christmas shop this year.

"Seemed to me a real good thing that she's looking for extra help, don't you agree, honey? Lillian's a strong woman. She'll hold that family together—you mark my words."

Jared Barnett didn't understand how a small town works, and I doubted he would realize what his lack of education might cost him.

CHAPTER NINE

Tuesday morning dragged by. Whether people were already off work and heading somewhere for the holiday or what, they certainly weren't calling me. I met a couple of other realtors for lunch for some networking. The relationships between real estate offices here in Serendipity was much more pleasant than I'd experienced in the city.

"Melissa, I heard about that guy Barnett. What a crazy idea he's got, huh? Can you imagine people building mansions like he's talking about here in our county?"

"No, not really. But he seemed to be convinced."

"I told him to his face that he was crazy. Not in a

hateful way, you know."

"I'm sure you were very subtle about it."

"Maybe not subtle, but you know, I sugar-coated it some. Thanks for thinking of us, we've all given it our consideration, and just so you know, the guys in white coats have been alerted to the make and model of your vehicle." He guffawed and slapped his knee.

I was glad to get out of there. Although I doubted the luxury development could happen, I wouldn't have shut Barnett down if the kind of property he wanted had been available. The conversation over lunch had been a reminder of the kind of narrow thinking that had stunted the growth of our county for years. With factories moving out or simply shutting down and nothing much new coming in, we needed to be looking for options, not throwing ideas out before they had a chance.

It made me angry and sad at the same time. Serendipity was a neat little town with a lot of potential, but we were very adept at ruining opportunities for ourselves.

I piddled around my office the rest of the

afternoon, and even did some housework carrying my phone in my pocket and listening for the doorbell. Just when I was ready to put the "Closed" sign in the door, the doorbell rang. Jim Standish was standing on the front porch peeking through the glass at me. I opened the door.

"Mel. We need to talk."

"Jim. Well, you look different." He was wearing a dark gray suit, white shirt, and a red necktie with tiny green Christmas trees woven into it.

"These are my work clothes for the day job."

"I'm not sure when I last saw you looking so dressed up."

"Maybe prom."

Did I need that? Had I actually somehow deserved that?

"Yeah, maybe prom. The night you ruined my life."

"That's ridiculous."

"The night you started ruining my life then. Let's see. Dump Melissa, marry Diana, get set up in the law firm, make big bucks, and be very happy."

"Mel, don't do this."

"Oh really? Why shouldn't I? What can I possibly hurt? Matthew isn't here, so as far as I know, I can say anything I want to you."

"Why not say it in front of Matthew?"

"Because he worships you. He loves you, Jim. Maybe you haven't noticed."

"Yeah, I noticed. Matthew is a great kid, and I wouldn't do anything to hurt him. Which is one reason you and I are having this discussion now."

"Your mom will wonder why I'm not there to pick him up on time."

"That's okay. She and Francie will keep him busy. They've got a million things to do this week, you know. It's almost the Christmas season." He was really shouting now. "Not that you care what that means to my family. All you care about is money and making a big name for yourself back here in the little hometown. What happened to you after you left here, Mel, to make you so cold-hearted?"

"Nothing happened to me after I left. It's what happened *before* I left that changed everything. *You* changed everything, Jim. Don't accuse me of being driven by money and making a name for myself. That's your own profile, isn't it? Except you had the trophy wife and her precious daddy to help you. Pretty neat set-up, and I'm sure glad you didn't let me get in the way of it. Little boring Mel, so love-struck. I would have followed you anywhere. And you broke up with me with no explanation at all, and rode into the sunset of success. Well, now that the trophy wife is gone and her daddy's law firm kicked you out, how's life treating you, Jim?"

Other than a muscle working overtime in his lower jaw, he looked completely calm.

"Life's not working out too well. I managed to live through that series of poor decisions and was getting along okay with my own small law office, and settled into my new little house on the farm, and then—boom—Dad died. And everything seemed to fall on me as the oldest son. But I worked hard and thought the family would get through okay. Then you showed up and I had the crazy idea that the two of us might make amends. I fell for Matthew, as if he were my own kid, and you and I had some moments. But what I hadn't realized was that all this time, as my mom babysat your son and you wormed your way back into our lives, you were scheming to ruin everything."

"What? What are you talking about?"

"I know about Barnett. I know you've been talking to him. He came to see me today, Mel, *after* he paid a visit to my mother. Do you know what that did to her? She considers you almost one of her own, you know. She kept telling me that Barnett wasn't being honest about his conversations with you. But I can see in your eyes that her trust in you is misplaced. You're representing him, aren't you? You're somehow working for him to get us to sell the farm. How can you do this?"

He stopped, took a deep breath, and continued, almost in a whisper.

"Mel. I was falling in love with you again. I thought—I thought we had a chance this time. That our lives were headed in the same direction at last."

He went out, leaving the door standing wide open. A cold November wind blew through me as Jim

Standish got into his blue pickup truck and drove away for the last time.

****

I pulled into the parking area by Lillian's house afraid of what my reception might be when I appeared to pick up Matthew. I parked, took a deep breath, and walked up the front porch steps. Francie opened the door before I could knock. She had obviously been crying. She stepped out onto the porch with me and closed the door silently.

"Mel? We're pretty confused here about what's going on. This Barnett guy, you know?"

"I understand—Jim told me the guy came out and talked to your mom. I can't believe his nerve."

"But—you didn't know what his plan was, right? He said you did. He said you had seen the drawings and thought it was great. But I know that can't be true." Her eyes were pleading.

"Francie, I had talked to the guy, but that's it. I don't represent him.

"Jim says you were trying to get us to sell. That you were getting close to our family—you know, like the old days—so we would listen to you when you were ready to spring this idea on us."

"Francie, how can you think for a minute that I'd do something like that?"

"I don't know what to think, Mel. You were gone, then you were back. You didn't keep in very good touch before, but suddenly you're here all the time. And Matthew—you know, he's stolen our hearts. We're so confused. This is such a horribly hard time for us right now, anyway...."

I put my arms around her and hugged her tight. What in the world was that Barnett guy trying to do here? Making me out to be some kind of infiltrator wasn't going to encourage the Standish family to sell. It was nuts.

Francie was crying for real now. "Mom says— maybe that's what people think about us. That we're just sitting on this property for no reason, and there's all this money to be made for the whole community, but we're not letting it happen. Mom says maybe we should just sell it and get out. I couldn't believe the words came out of her mouth. I really couldn't. It's like her heart was broken all over again."

"I'm not a perfect friend, but I would never, never push Lillian to sell this land. Now with your dad gone, the farm represents a lot to her. I remember Harry talking about how the farm started, that he had inherited it when his dad died. And since he and Lillian loved Christmas so much, they planted a few trees. And over the years, they just kept planting and buying little bits of land to add to the property, and eventually that was the entire farm. They were original thinkers, because this was the first Christmas tree farm in the area. I think they're the first entrepreneurs I was ever aware of."

"Mostly I have just taken it for granted until lately."

"Sure, because you were raised here. That's human nature."

"It's cool that you remember Mom and Dad's story."

"They're important to me. Your whole family is so special to me, Francie." I put her away from me, shaking her a little. "Francie, honey, wake up and smell the wassail."

She looked at me, blinked, and started to giggle. "Wake up and smell the *wassail*?"

"Honey, it's two days before Thanksgiving. Besides the fact that Jared Barnett is one of the smoothest liars to grace our fair town, the other big news is that we have a Christmas season to get through. Or maybe I should say, we have a Christmas season to bring to our county. Isn't that the way your dad looked at it? He was just a few pounds and a flowing white beard shy of being Father Christmas himself. I don't want to let him down, that's for sure."

Francie hiccupped some leftover tears.

"None of us wants to let Dad down. I worry about Mom...."

"Which is why I need to go inside and talk to her. Okay, Francie?"

Lillian was more jangled than angry. She hadn't wanted to believe Barnett, and when she had called Jim about it, he had immediately sided with the liar.

Wow, that rankled. Did he hate me so much?

Francie took Matthew over to "work" in the Christmas shop for a little while so I could talk to Lillian. I knelt by her chair.

"Lillian, there is no way I would try to push you into selling the farm. If you wanted to sell, sure I'd be glad to assist in whatever way was appropriate. Barnett and Jim would be quick to point out that I could make a tidy sum working on the deal. But whether or not to sell, whenever, is entirely your call. You and your kids have to decide the right thing to do here, for all of you."

"Melissa honey, I didn't want to believe it. I shouldn't have let Jim—That boy. When will he ever learn?"

I wondered the same thing myself. One minute Jim was falling in love with me and the next minute he was accusing me of high treason against Christmas. Somebody was conflicted, and in a big way.

Lillian went to the kitchen sink and washed away the signs of crying, dried her face with a paper towel. "Well. I have a Thanksgiving dinner to start. It's Tuesday night, for goodness sake." She picked up a wooden spoon and gestured me toward the door.

"Honey, you and Matthew be sure and arrive Thursday by 11:30. I have a feeling this Christmas season is going to start even earlier than usual."

I checked with Francie and Matthew. They assured me that they had loads of work to do, and wouldn't miss me if I needed to run an unexpected errand.

Instead of turning around and going down the driveway to Tree Farm Road, I put the SUV into four-wheel drive and headed toward the trees. I was pretty sure I saw Francie's face in the Christmas shop window as I went past, and that now she was giving me a thumbs-up.

CHAPTER TEN

It took a little longer than I expected, but I managed to find my way to Jim's house. Years ago when we were dating he had brought me up here, stepped off the size of the house he would build for us. We'd be happy here, in our cozy little log home. I'd help on the farm and he would work in a law firm. We'd have two kids—a girl who looked like me and a boy who looked like him. Yep, we had it all figured out. But one of us had decided to chuck our plans.

I pounded on his door until he opened it. In jeans, flannel shirt, and sock-footed, he looked comfortable and angry at the same time.

"What do you want?" he growled.

I stood in the doorway with my arms crossed. "How about honesty? That would be different."

"Meaning?"

"Start with why you suddenly dumped me in high school, and then finish by telling me why *in the world* you would believe a desperate real estate developer over me. Don't worry about trying to spare my feelings, because apparently I don't have any."

He sighed and I swear his shoulders sagged six inches.

"Come inside, Mel." He didn't wait to see if I did it or not, just walked away and dropped into a big rocking chair by the cold fireplace. I followed him in, closed the door behind me, and perched on the hearth directly in front of him.

"I'm waiting." Seething was more like it. I tried not to tap my foot to hurry him up.

"Yeah." He scratched his jaw. "Remember when I told you about this cabin? About how I was going to build it for us?"

"Of course."

"I was going to be a lawyer and we would have

two kids, and—do you remember what you were going to do?"

"Of course. I was going to work on the tree farm."

He grimaced. "Right. What if we had followed that little plan? Would you have even gone to college?"

"Well…sure. I had those scholarships." I had wanted to go to college, but also wanted to marry Jim and have a happy home. The main thing I needed at the time was to be away from my parents, making my own life one way or another. I had thought Jim and I could make it work.

"I don't think you would have gone to college, Mel. Carla and—oh, I can never remember that guy's name—the guy she went to the prom with, you know?"

I nodded.

"The four of us, at prom, while we were eating, got to talking about after graduation. That guy said he was off to Purdue to study pharmacy, Carla said she would go to design school. I talked about being a lawyer. And you just sat there and smiled."

"And that's a bad thing?"

"Mel, you had so much going for you. You were

the smartest one in our class, but you were ready to settle down and be happy."

"You obviously couldn't let that happen." I crossed my arms, angry with him for trying to make this my fault.

"I wasn't prepared for that kind of commitment—not yet. There you were, ready to get married right away and start making those two kids. I had college to get through, and then law school. I loved you, to the extent an eighteen year old knows about love. But it scared me to death for you to talk that way. I was intent on starting my new life. College and career first, wife and family later on. I wanted to do those things, you know? Everything we had talked about. But we hadn't given it a timeframe while we were dreaming it, and things were happening too fast for me. You were so good and sweet, but I was suddenly looking for a way out."

"Enter Diana." Whom I could still picture in her bikini, high heels, and smug grin. It still made me a little nauseous.

"Diana had been flirting with me for years." He

shrugged. "When you're on the football team, it happens. That night in the gym, with the fake waterfall making that weird sound and all of us talking about our futures, I realized something needed to happen, and fast. Diana and Greg showing up at the party was a surprise, but it set some stuff in motion."

"Stuff like lust?" I asked sweetly.

He frowned and leaned forward. "Diana—Diana was desperate. She had made a lot of mistakes in high school, and her dad basically gave her an ultimatum to shape up or he'd cut off any funds. Let her go out into the world on her own and see if she grew up. She saw me as a way to make amends with the old man, and for the most part it worked. Of course, I had always known him. He liked me, thought I would do well as a lawyer. He also could pull strings. I had some internships I would never have gotten otherwise."

"Not that it mattered in the end, of course. I came back to Serendipity to practice. Diana and I had the biggest wedding of the year, and the ugliest divorce of the decade. No matter what I did, she was never happy. She was always out with friends, female and male. If I questioned her, she got defensive and hateful. I would never have believed how spiteful she could become." He shook his head. "When the divorce and property settlement were done, I came out here to the farm and built the house I always intended to build."

I looked around for a moment at the living room. It was the way I had pictured it all those years ago.

He stood and started to pace. "You never needed me, Mel. You just thought you did. My family had become like a second family to you, and marrying me would make it official."

"What a horrible thing to say." I should never have confided in him about the ugliness of my own family after keeping it to myself all these years.

"But true. More true, in fact, than I knew at the time. Because of the way you were brought up, you didn't believe in yourself, that you could do great things on your own. I pushed you away out of selfishness. If I had known back then, on prom night, how your parents had treated you, maybe I would have done things differently, found another way instead of the Diana 'out.' I don't know." He smacked a door frame with his hand. "The best thing that happened is you went out into the world and made your own life."

Jim reached over and touched that dang cleft in my chin for just a second. "You thought you needed me, and my family, but you just needed to believe in yourself. You're amazing, Mel. I've always known that, even if you haven't."

It made sense. Some of it was very convoluted thinking, but we'd been teenagers, so what can you expect? By pure dumb luck—coincidence?—serendipity—due to Jim's breaking up with me, I had discovered my own strength and abilities. I felt the hurt and anger I'd held all this time start to fall away.

"And today when you believed I would go behind your back and work with Jared Barnett to make a great business deal...?"

"That was me being defensive. I love having you back here, Mel. And Matthew has given us all a better outlook. I was afraid that, just when I could believe you and I might have a future together after all, you were using the past against me."

"Which you deserved."

He hung his head a little. "Yeah, probably."

"So, Jim, what will it take to convince you that I wasn't doing something underhanded?"

"That Barnett guy himself, it looks like. Earlier this evening I got a call from Dean Williams. Seems a stranger named Jared came in for a haircut and was asking a lot of personal questions about my family, and about you too. Dean didn't trust the guy, and tonight when he was talking to Alice about it, she suggested he call me. Soon as I hung up with Dean, Mom called and reamed me out. That would have happened after you talked to her and Francie."

"So you broke up with me because I was terrific, and when I came back to town you deemed me untrustworthy." His twisted logic was maddening. I could only imagine he was a great lawyer.

"Sorry, Mel. I've built up some pretty strong defenses for myself and my family. Even more so since Dad died.

"Oh, Jim. I know you're hurting too. You were always so close to him."

"I talked to him most every day of my life 'til he

died. Even in college and law school. We were really tight, and I miss him like hell."

"I'm sure he would be proud of the work you've done this year to keep everything going, and how good you are to your mom. Their dream of this farm came true through hard work. Driving up here, I got a glimmer of an idea that might be a nice little change-up for everybody in your family."

"What?"

I held up a hand. "Not yet. I have to think it through more thoroughly, do a little research. But right now I need to pick up Matthew and get him to bed." I stood up. "Good night, Jim."

"Night, Mel. You don't hate me anymore, right?"

"Right. I could maybe warm up to you a bit, but it will require more effort on your part."

He brightened. "I will take that under advisement, Ms. Singer, and present my findings to you in a timely manner."

"Oh please, no lawyer talk."

I was smiling the whole drive back down to the Christmas shop. What a weird series of circumstances had brought Jim and me to this point from the pool party at the Osbornes all those years ago. But I had to admit I had gained a lot in the years, even though I felt I had been so badly wronged.

I had worked hard and excelled in college, sought out my career, and made a name for myself there too. I had been in a few relationships, but none of them had that forever feeling. If I'm honest, I was looking for someone like Jim, and never found him. So when I decided I was ready to be a mom, I did all the stuff necessary to get an *in vitro* fertilization from an anonymous donor. The selection process was pretty cool. Kind of like an online dating profile, only different. I think I'm a pretty good mom, though as expected, single parenting is a challenge.

I picked Matthew up at the shop and got us home as soon as I could. I snuggled into bed with him, feeling happier because I understood my past a little better. I sang my usual lullaby, but instead of falling asleep, he patted my cheek.

"Mommy, I'm gonna sleep in my truck bed tonight." He picked up his little piece of blanket and went into his room across the hall. I didn't want to jinx things by following him in there, so I just tiptoed to the door, which was ajar. He was humming softly to himself, lying on his side toward the wall where the colorful trucks were painted.

Funny how Matthew had found a bit of independence tonight, just a little while after Jim had explained his concern years ago that I wouldn't find mine.

CHAPTER ELEVEN

Thanksgiving lunch was amazing. There was so much food we almost didn't get the leftovers poked into Lillian's big fridge. I looked at the clock and decided I had plenty of time to share my ideas with everyone. Lillian and all four children were there—Jim, Carla, Francie, and David who had a couple days' start on his annual Christmas season beard. Matthew played on the floor with Harry's wooden truck, hauling some twigs back and forth. Daisy lay near him, watching carefully.

I stood in the center of the room, looking around at all of them, and cleared my throat.

"Since we're all here together and the frenzy hasn't

quite begun, I wonder if we could take a few minutes to discuss the future of the farm."

Lillian nodded and sat a little straighter in her chair.

"I understand you all care about the farm and want to continue Harry's dream. I also understand it's more than you can physically do."

I looked at Francie. "Your heart isn't here, honey, much as you love your family. If you end up staying in Serendipity, you'll always be a little bit unhappy, and nobody wants that. I think you've had plenty of unhappiness already."

"Of course, she isn't going to stay in Serendipity. Her husband would never want to live here. We all know Brad well enough to know that," David huffed.

"Well, Brad does have a successful legal practice—" Francie began.

"And he wouldn't want to go into a partnership with our dear brother Jim," said David, rolling his eyes. "So Francie moves on when Mom's ready for her to go. But what about her piece of the land?"

"You can sell it, if you need to, to support the

farm."

Francie was wringing her hands.

"Harry wouldn't want us to do that," said Lillian decisively.

"No. I know he wouldn't, Mom. But if the money is needed, I'm offering." Francie looked around at the stricken faces of her siblings.

David stood. "I'm sorry I mentioned your corner of the farm, Francie. I always come off sounding heartless, but really I'm just painfully blunt. I don't want you to give up your inheritance. Dad gave each of us a piece of the land, and that's yours."

"Selling off one corner of the farm isn't any kind of an answer. It decreases the value of the rest and wouldn't realize much in the way of quick money." I touched her shoulder, smiled at her. "It's good of you to be so unselfish, Francie."

"I don't know what to do to actually help."

"I want to talk to you about an opportunity that might be the answer we've been looking for." I didn't correct the fact that I included myself in that. My developing relationship with Jim gave me a bigger emotional stake than ever concerning the Standish family and their farm.

"I've spent some time with Mrs. Jenson who owns the B&B in town. She keeps pretty busy with that. Sometimes there are more calls than she has rooms. Sometimes the people who call have something in particular in mind and she doesn't have what they want, so they hang up and find another place to go. We're talking about people who just want to get away, not those who have a particular interest in spending time in Serendipity."

"Yeah. There aren't a lot of people in that second category," David offered unhelpfully.

I wagged a finger at him. "More than you might think, but we'll get to them. So anyway she fields calls from people who are celebrating an anniversary and want a private setting. Something cozy and intimate. Most of her rooms share a bath, and the one that doesn't is still right there with everybody else in a big, old house with creaky floors. Mrs. Jenson's place doesn't cater to people who want a romantic getaway. Get the picture?"

Carla shot me a wink showing she knew what I was hinting at.

I plodded on, afraid of losing momentum. "She also gets calls from people she's met at statewide church meetings, who know she has a B&B. These people are looking for a place for a spiritual retreat. Much as she tries to accommodate everyone, she can't host a religious retreat among her other patrons. Besides the fact that she simply doesn't have that much space."

Jim shook his head. "I'm listening, honest, but sure don't have any idea why we're talking about Mrs. Jenson's B&B."

I looked at him, hands on my hips. "Because that's the opportunity."

"What is?" Jim still looked confused.

"A B&B. Right here on the tree farm," I announced and hoped my smile was encouraging.

David frowned. "Mom likes people, but she doesn't need to have strangers wandering in and out of the house. I wouldn't be comfortable with that happening, to be honest."

"How sweet, David." Lillian smiled at him, then turned to me. "It might be interesting to try it, Melissa. I've never given any thought to running a bed and breakfast."

Bless her heart. She was an adaptable lady.

"I wasn't necessarily suggesting that you have people stay here in the house with you, Lillian. If you did, you would have a similar clientele that Mrs. Jenson does, and as I was saying, she isn't able to meet the needs of some people."

"So what you're suggesting is...?" Lillian leaned forward eagerly.

"Mini barns. Not exactly mini barns, but you know the ones you see for sale at the hardware stores and such?" I looked around to make sure everyone was following. "Something a bit bigger than that, and trimmed out so it has more of a cabin look. A tiny bathroom and kitchen area, and there you go—private little getaway for a romantic weekend, or spiritual retreat, tucked into a beautiful pine forest."

"Put mini barns all over the farm?" Jim looked as if he were trying to picture the result.

"Not every few feet," I assured him. "But spread around the acreage."

"Huh. Well, we've got the lanes for people to drive back. Just need a little more gravel on some of them." He was giving the idea a chance, thank goodness.

I smiled at him, grateful. "Don't make it too perfect. Part of the draw will be the backwoods feel of it."

David looked relieved at that, as if he had expected to shovel gravel.

"Might put one or two cabins near the lake," Jim said, considering.

"We'll have to get the building inspector to sign off on this," said David. "Whatever we do will have to have plumbing, electricity, septic system. Sounds like a lot of money to spend for something we don't know the return on."

Francie laughed at him. "David, you know this will be a draw. You're an example of the kind of people who would come up from Louisville on the weekends. They work hard, maybe travel for their job, and by the end of the week they just want quiet and relaxation.

Hey—I live in the city, remember. I know what that's like."

David looked thoughtful, no doubt doing some mental math.

I appreciated Francie's contribution. "That's the kind of thing that really made sense to me about Jared Barnett's idea. I know this wouldn't be everyone's idea of a perfect weekend, but think of the magazines you read and the kinds of vacations that are touted. So many that have a taste of quiet and nature are in national parks, or at the least in state parks. The state parks in Indiana don't all have cabins, so they're still not reaching the people who want to be out in nature, yet not camping."

"We could offer camping too, I guess," Francie said cautiously.

"Do you want to get into that?" David's deep frown was back. "More danger of fire I'd say, because campers like to have the option of building a campfire."

"No campground," Jim said emphatically. "One hot dry summer and an unsupervised campfire and the whole place, including our homes, could go up in flames."

"I just realized what I could do," said Lillian. "The Christmas shop could be used in the off season as the place for our guests to come and have breakfast. That could be included in the fee, right? I would know how many people are staying each night, since I'm taking the money and handing out the keys. Somebody can draw a nice map for me to hand out. And each morning I'll serve breakfast in the Christmas shop. Casseroles, biscuits and gravy, fresh fruit in season. It could be fun. Sometimes since you all went out on your own, I miss cooking for a crowd."

Carla looked at Lillian. "You sure that wouldn't be too much on you, Mom? We don't want you to overdo."

"I'm not sick, honey. I'm grieving—we're all grieving. But Melissa, and everybody, help me understand how this would make the farm more sustainable."

"We would get a loan to do the improvements. I don't think that'll be a problem at all," said Jim. "We advertise—"

"I'll be in charge of that," David offered.

"Great. We advertise, we get people in here, they tell their friends. The money they spend will pay back the loan."

Now we were on a roll. "And the increased income will free up some money so you can hire someone, or more than one, to help Jim do the pruning."

"And the mowing. Most of the grunt work is in the summer. Might be a decent summer job for a couple of high school kids who don't mind working hard." He slapped his forehead. "I should have gotten more help this year, but I just toughed it out. Sometimes I'm too hard headed."

"Only sometimes?" asked David.

"You're like your father, Jim, in that you try to do it all yourself." Lillian looked slowly around the room, making careful eye contact with each of her children, and also with me. "That's not a good way to run a business, and we won't be doing it that way anymore. We can't let Jim keep carrying more than his share of the work. I love the idea of giving jobs to high school students."

"They'll be fighting over who gets to run the big fancy mower," Carla chuckled.

"Maybe," said Jim. "We'll see what happens. Good idea."

"What do you think about letting people stay in the cabins in the winter? Might get in the way of our main business, right?" David asked

"The overnight guests will mostly be inside the cabins, there will be one, maybe two vehicles parked outside each one. If guests want to walk in the woods, that doesn't hurt anything, right?"

Jim shook his head.

"So the B&B users won't be in the way of tree customers to any great extent."

"I think people would love staying here during cold weather," said Francie. "It's a short trip from Louisville for the change of pace, and if there are kids they can see how the Christmas tree farm works."

"What about breakfast for them when the Christmas shop is set up for the retail season though? That won't work," David said.

"Maybe I'll serve breakfast in the house then. I'll

have to think about it. Or drive around to the cabins and deliver breakfast. That might be an option. I know a friendly dog who would love to go with me and announce our arrival at each place."

Carla winced. "That might not be quite what people want, if they're here for a romantic weekend, Mom."

I laughed. "These are things we can fine-tune later, everybody. The question right now is, do you want to pursue the possibilities of little cabins scattered through the property as extra income?"

"It's worlds better than selling to a developer who would destroy the farm, take down most of the trees, and replace them with big houses," said Francie. "Then, of course, name the development Piney Acres. Gag."

Carla laughed. "I love the idea of being able to keep the farm and the Christmas tree business, but having something else going on too. I think it could be a lot of fun to decorate the interiors of the little cabins." I could see she was envisioning décor already. "We could have some that are particularly romantic, say, and if someone calls for a honeymoon or anniversary, we'd know which ones to suggest."

"Put pictures online. Start a website. Put flyers in the State welcome centers." David was getting into it now.

"Advertise in magazines that target this area," Francie offered.

"Don't go crazy with lots of paid advertising," I cautioned. "Join the State B&B association and see what perks go along with membership. I know you get listed on their website with a link to your own, if you have one, because I looked up the local B&B. She isn't interested in having a site of her own, but gets some referrals that way."

David had found an envelope and was furiously scribbling notes. "Try to get some Louisville media attention. One of the news anchors always comes up here to cut his own tree. He would be a good contact for that."

By the time the first Christmas tree customer showed up, we were ready. We had some hope—hope that not only would we get through this Christmas season, which had seemed such an insurmountable task a few weeks ago, but that we might be able to keep the farm going in the future, too.

CHAPTER TWELVE

A couple of weeks into the season, Alice stopped at my house shortly before closing time.

"Hey."

"Hi, Alice. This is a surprise."

"Yes. To me, as well." She raised the cardboard carrier I hadn't noticed when she walked in.

"Coffee?"

"Hot cocoa from The Chocolate Muffin."

"Oh, wow. Come right on in. Good thing that place wasn't open when we were kids. I would have weighed three hundred pounds and been spoiled for any other bakery in the world." I was disappointed she hadn't brought any pastries, but the cocoa was amazing. "Have a seat." She sat on the big sectional and I sat facing her. "Thanks for the cocoa. I only have a few minutes though. I have to leave to pick up Matthew. Assuming no potential clients come in right before closing."

"Mel, I know you're pressed for time. I'm going to work some this evening too." She took a deep breath and seemed to be at war with herself. "I try really hard not to gossip. I hate the gossip in this town—it is always tearing people down. But Dean shared something with me that I thought you should know."

"Okay."

"You know he's a barber and he had a run-in with that guy who was trying to pressure the Standishes into selling?"

"Um, yes."

"Dean was really riled up about that."

"Okay."

"He was very angry and full of righteous indignation on behalf of the Standish family—Jim in particular. Partly because they went to school together, partly because he's a customer and an occasional fishing buddy. But also partly because Jim was very badly wronged by another gold digger in the past."

"Um, Alice. None of my business here." I took a big drink of cocoa and immediately scalded my mouth.

"Yes it's your business. You and Jim have a history. And I think you have a future as well."

"Maybe. Jury's still out…"

"Here's the thing, Mel. Several years ago, David and Jim and Dean, and Dean's buddy Irv and maybe somebody else went on a camping and fishing trip. Evidently out by the campfire one night they started sharing stories. Most guys from Serendipity in that age group are dads. But these four aren't, and they started talking about it. Who knows how much beer had been consumed, but Jim really loosened up and said he and Diana were trying to have a baby—"

I stood up, almost toppling the hot cocoa on the low table. "Alice—time out. This is nothing I want to hear about, trust me."

"Yes, it is, Mel. Have a seat."

Alice is always very soft spoken, always asks and never tells. I sat.

"Diana said she was doing all the right herbal teas and relaxation and whatever to try to get pregnant, and normal methods—sorry—normal methods weren't getting it. The doctor told her the only way was to try *in vitro*. They go to the city and the sperm is collected. Evidently, there was some kind of preparation Diana was supposed to undergo before implantation. And she made the appointment at a time when Jim had a jury trial, so he couldn't go with her."

My throat was super dry, wondering where this story was going, and if I'd be in any shape to hear the ending of it.

"Long story short, it was all a ruse. She had no intention of getting pregnant. And for some reason, she hated Jim so much that she *sold his sperm to a sperm bank.*"

"She—are you serious?" I had never liked Diana, but this was beyond anything I could have imagined.

Alice nodded. "Of course I'm serious. I don't have a clue how you'd go about doing that. Seems like you'd need the donor's permission. Gah! Well, when she left Jim, in addition to all the other ugliness of the divorce, she laid this news on him." Alice swatted at a tear that had escaped and started to run down her face. "He wanted kids so much, and to know that she had lied to him about it and then sold his sperm."

I sat down by Alice and put my arm around her. This was more painful to her than I would have expected.

She took a deep breath. "Well, Jim has been dealing with all that trauma for a few years, and then his dad died. I just thought you might want to know."

"So I'll be more understanding?" It was a huge burden for him to have carried alone.

"Mel, come on. Hello—*Matthew*."

"Matthew?"

"You never said who his dad is."

"No, I didn't."

"I'm listening, if you want to tell me a story now about a wonderful guy who would have been a great dad but somehow was tragically killed on a mission trip to take medicine to some starving children."

Her eyes were intense but they weren't searching for an answer. She knew the answer, and I had never told a single soul.

"How, Alice? How did you know this about Matthew?"

She smiled gently. "I have no idea. Maybe because you and I have been friends since almost babyhood." She stood and smoothed her jeans. "I just didn't realize until Dean told me this story, that Jim is Matthew's dad. Pretty strange coincidence, huh?

"If you want to use the word coincidence. And we certainly don't know that Jim is Matthew's dad."

"They look identical. I bet if you asked Lillian to see pictures of Jim at that age—I'm sure Lillian has noticed but didn't say anything. Anyway, as far as I know, you and I and good old Diana are the only females to know Jim's story. And only you and I know your story. I'm not going to tell anybody anything…but I think you should."

I started to disagree but she just shook her head and smiled again.

"Think about it, Mel. I know you'll choose the right path."

CHAPTER THIRTEEN

Tree season was going well, according to the Standishes. There were lots of customers, but plenty of help too. The weather was mostly decent, and when it turned cold or snowed a little, there were more customers, just as expected.

I heard from Carla that Emily's dad drove up one afternoon in his old pick-up truck. He reported Emily was doing better than the doctors had expected. His plan was to buy a big tree for their home as usual, and also take a small one to Emily's room at the rehab facility. David and Jim helped him choose, cut, and load the trees, and flatly refused payment. Lillian assembled a little bag of goodies from the Christmas shop when she realized what was going on, and hugged the appreciative man when handing it to him.

"Send us a picture of your girl enjoying that tree," Jim had said gruffly, and Emily's dad promised to do so. That, Carla said, is just how their father would have handled it.

The Friday morning before Christmas, I got a text from Jim. Francie had given him my cell number. He asked me to go out with him after the farm and shop closed for the night. Carla would drive Matthew home, put him to bed, and stay with him until I got back.

He had everything organized, which was sweet, and I appreciated his effort. I wondered if he would regret it all after we hashed out the things that remained between us.

A cold drizzle started to fall about an hour before closing, effectively stopping the traffic. Jim came into the Christmas shop.

"Hey."

"Hey." Why was I so nervous? This felt like the most awkward first date ever.

"Weather forecast says this won't clear up tonight. David can handle things outside, if you think the boss will let you leave a little early." He sent Lillian a winning smile.

"I suppose," she said. Clearly, Lillian was happy to see the possibility of Jim and me getting back together even after so much time had passed. She glanced at Matthew, who was sitting at the little desk they had created for him near the cash register. He was "counting" his play money. "Yes, it seems things are under control here. You children have a nice evening. See you tomorrow?" This question was directed at me.

"I hope so. I feel the need to have the office open in the morning, just in case. But I'll be out here as soon as I can."

"You do what's best for yourself, Melissa. I mean that." She turned then and went to check a display of Christmas sock monkeys. But I wondered if there was more than one meaning to her statement. Was she afraid I would fall in with Jim without thinking through everything?

Jim stood beside me, looking around at the

Christmas shop.

"Look around you, Melissa," he said softly. "You and Matthew have made this possible. Before you came back to Serendipity, our family was really struggling. We still are, of course, but we're getting our feet under us at last. Look at Francie. See what she's wearing over those designer jeans and cashmere sweater? Dad's favorite old Carhartt jacket. She's worn it every day since the weather turned cool. Sure, she and Brad have lived in Florida, and you can imagine her blood has thinned some. But if you give her a big hug you'll smell Dad's aftershave mixed with pine from the trees."

"Francie tells me Brad is flying up to have Christmas here, and Joseph is going to be here too. That will be so good for her. She's sacrificed a lot. You all have."

He shrugged. "It's family. You do what needs doing. Like Carla over there giving decorating advice and enjoying herself. She doesn't feel like she has to give up her work, or spend less time at her shop to work with me on the trees. She *would* do it, if we needed her to. That's the point."

Jim tipped his head toward the door where trees were sold and tied onto vehicles. "David's not exactly in his element here, but he also doesn't mind giving these few weeks to the farm. It makes him feel better about living away all year and not really contributing much in the way of physical labor. Plus, in my opinion, he just likes the excuse not to shave for a month straight." He chuckled. "And now he's going to be able to lend his marketing expertise to the new life of the farm."

Jim looked around slyly, then snatched a little bag of chocolate chip cookies off the counter and slid it into his pocket. "And Mom. She's really in her element, isn't she? Working here in the shop, and thinking about how the B&B will work. If Dad were alive, we might not have needed the B&B, but we also wouldn't have thought of it without you. You've done us such a favor."

He sighed. "What a gift you've given us all, helping us look at our situation in a different way. I wish Dad could see us now. I think he'd be happy to know that even though we're missing him like hell, we're figuring out our road from here." He took my hand gently. "Too bad he and Matthew never got to meet. Matthew's such a trip, and I know Dad would have loved having him around. Would have taught him stuff about the farm, if he wanted to learn."

I squeezed his hand. It was such a blessing to be accepted by this family.

"I wish Matthew could have met Harry too. Your dad was so good and kind, and so much fun."

"Yes he was." Jim sighed. "Okay, Ms. Singer, I'm going to sweep you off your feet tonight. Let's stop talking about work."

CHAPTER FOURTEEN

Jim followed me home in his truck and waited while I parked in my garage. Then I climbed into his pickup with him.

"Have you been to the Barbeque Basement?"

"Um, no. I've heard of it though."

"Best barbeque in Serendipity."

"Also the only barbeque in Serendipity?"

"Well, yeah, unless people are grilling in their yards. It's great stuff though. Some reviewer from the Louisville Courier-Journal came up and gave it a glowing write-up, so there are always crowds."

Jim parked in a municipal lot just off the town

square, because the small lot behind the restaurant and all the street parking was full. We went in the back door of what had previously been a shoe and clothing store. But instead of going into that portion of the building where I'd shopped as a kid for shoes, we went down the dark stairway into a huge rock-and-brick-walled basement. The white ceiling was heavily textured, so it reminded me of stalactites. The floor was concrete and brick, and there was a rough wood bar along one wall. The tables and chairs were sturdy but certainly not fancy. A little stage on the far end was empty for the moment except for the band's instruments. They seemed to be taking a break at the bar. We had to wait a few minutes for a table, and it was in the middle of everything. The food was delicious, and the craft beer selection immense, but there was no chance for private conversation, or much of any conversation at all, once the band started playing. They were very talented though, and the whole experience reminded me of prom because of the loud music and funky décor. They were lacking a fake waterfall and grass huts, but still.

"I enjoyed that," I said when we were outside in

the cold fresh air again. "Such an unusual place, and so busy."

"Like I said, people come up from Louisville. I'd guess twenty percent or more of tonight's crowd wasn't local."

"I wonder if the management would let you put up some kind of advertisement about the tree farm. Next year, I mean. Might bring in a few customers from that area, and you know word of mouth."

"Yeah. Word of mouth, good or bad, makes all the difference. But that's a good idea. You're always thinking, aren't you, Mel?"

"I guess. Just trying to help."

"Hey—I didn't mean that to sound negative. It is a good idea, and you've had lots of them. I appreciate it. We all appreciate it."

"Maybe it's easier to look at things with the farm from a little bit outside like I do. I'd think it would be difficult to imagine changes from your perspective. Your focus this year especially is to honor Harry. That's admirable."

"No big deal. It's just who we are."

We were at the passenger side of the truck.

"Mel, I'm really out of practice at dating, and of all things, I don't want to mess up when we're trying to start over. What do you want to do now?"

"In the old days we would have hung out with our friends, gone bowling or to the drive-in theater. Or parked on the farm and made out," I said, smiling up at him.

"Now there's an option."

I laughed. "That's good to know. I wonder if the old zing is still there."

I didn't have to wonder long, because he leaned down and gently kissed my lips. The electric pulse surely wasn't all weather-related static. I responded, and then his arms were around me, holding me as if I were the most precious person in the world to him.

"Oh, Mel," he said into my hair. "I can't believe you're here. I'm so thankful we have a chance to start over." He opened the door for me to climb in, then closed it softly. And sure enough, he drove us back to the farm, but this time to the northwest corner where his neat cabin sat.

"We can sit in the truck and make out, or go indoors and make out."

"Is there a possibility of going indoors and talking?"

He groaned. "We already talked." He got out of the truck and opened my door. "Okay, I guess. You're the company, so if you want to talk instead, we can. Is this going to be a habit?" He unlocked the cabin door and opened it for me. "Or do you think there's still a future for something more physical?"

"Oh, I'd say there's a great future for it. But we still have some things to iron out between us. More than I realized."

"What does that mean?" He turned on the gas log fire. "Something to drink?"

"Um. No thanks. I'm fine." I sat on the couch this time, facing the fire, and Jim sat next to me, and pulled my hands into his.

"What is it, Mel? You're worried about something."

"Jim, you and I have taken different paths to get here. I'm glad now I understand why you literally pushed me down my own path. But nonetheless, we've made decisions that brought us from nearly this exact location years ago, back here tonight. We could put it down to coincidence maybe, but I'm not much of a believer in coincidences. So I think there's an important reason you and I are here now."

"I hope it's making out, at the very least."

He said it so deadpan, I laughed out loud.

"I need to tell you something about Matthew. I haven't shared it with many people. Carla and Francie don't even know."

"Matthew? Is he sick? Can I help somehow?"

"Oh—my goodness. No, he isn't sick." I stood up and started to pace, needing the distance.

"It's more about Matthew's dad."

"He wants visitation?"

"Um. Well, no. He doesn't even know he's Matthew's dad." I felt my face getting hot. "I became pregnant with Matthew through *in vitro* fertilization. I went to a clinic and filled out a profile and from the possibilities, I chose this nice sounding donor. Never saw a name or where he lived, and I didn't care. I wanted to be a mom, and I have never regretted my decision."

"Good for you. You're a terrific mom. I wanted kids so much. Diana—she didn't."

We looked at each other for a minute or more. I had hoped Jim would pick up on my line of reasoning, but it seemed I'd have to spell it all out—without letting him know I had been told what Diana had done.

I took a deep breath. "Since coming back to Serendipity, I've noticed several things about Matthew that remind me of you. Sometimes the two of you will look at me, and it's like he's a smaller version of you. Isn't that funny?"

Jim frowned. "Funny?"

"Well, yes. Don't you think so?"

"I would call it something else. Maybe a miracle." He cleared his throat. "Diana said she couldn't get pregnant, and that she wanted to. We were going *in vitro*. But instead of going to the doctor to get the sperm implanted, she sold it. At least, that's what she said she did. I haven't been able to corroborate it at all, and I've tried." He hung his head. "She really hated me a lot.

Still does, as far as I know."

"Why?"

"She said our marriage was a lie. That I had only married her—used her—to further my career. She said..." He rubbed his hand over his stubbled jaw. "She said I was still in love with you."

"But you weren't."

"Diana got a lot of things wrong, but about that one thing, she was right."

"Oh, wow. And I thought I had suffered."

"We all did. You, me, Diana. What a mess."

"We survived. And about Matthew. I don't expect you to do anything different. He's crazy about you as it is."

"I'd like to have DNA testing done. If Matthew is my son, I want to do right by him, and by you, Mel. Looks like my good intentions sent us on an awful long road to come right back where we started."

I stopped pacing, sat down next to him. "I'm okay with the DNA testing, after Christmas sometime when life slows down. And the long road? I'm glad for that. It surprises me, but I really am glad. I came back to

Serendipity to make a name for myself, in a town where I felt I'd been mistreated by gossip as a teenager. I bought the Osborne house because it would give me control over the memory of prom night. But being here has helped me realize I was already a person I could be proud of, and I had already risen above the pain of the past by making my own life."

"Meaning you don't need me anymore, like you did?"

"Exactly, Jim. I don't need you the way I did." I slipped my hand into his. "I need you the way I do now. I like this equal footing better, and I have you to thank for that. You and your twisted teenage logic."

"Is this a good time for celebratory making out, do you think?"

I moved into his arms and kissed him. Even kissing was better now than it had been when we were young. Our relationship had progressed immensely—in spite of, and partly because of, the years we'd been apart.

CHAPTER FIFTEEN

From that evening on, there wasn't a night that I didn't fall asleep with a smile on my face. Every night after Matthew was tucked in, I snuggled into my bed with my phone and had a long conversation with Jim. We talked about books and movies and travel, hopes and fears, and plans for the future. Hesitation was out the window. We knew who we were and where we were going. And that, finally, we were going there together.

The joy of the Christmas season was multiplied for me this year because of being so happy in every facet of my life. But a part of me still worried about Lillian,

Francie, Carla, David and Jim who were facing this most important holiday of their family's life, for the first time without Harry.

Christmas Eve dawned cold and clear. Today would be relatively quiet since most people already had their trees. But there were always a few, Lillian said, who waited until Christmas Eve.

"Who am I to question? It's their tradition. We all have our own, don't we?"

Francie's husband Brad and their son Joseph had arrived the previous evening and were staying with Lillian too in the big house. They both put on work clothes and boots and pitched in where they were needed. The farm closed for the season on Christmas Eve at six.

The time came and no customers remained outside. Joseph and Brad, David and Jim gathered up the tools and put them into the box of Jim's truck, so he could take them home to sharpen, oil, and whatever was needed. Next year the tools would be in good shape.

Next year there would indeed be another Christmas on the Standish tree farm.

The guys came into the Christmas shop and helped extinguish pine-scented candles and unplug light displays. Carla was emptying the cash register, and Lillian walked around tidying as she did each evening. Francie shut off the CD player that had piped music inside and out for all those weeks.

That's when we heard it, sung so softly in a child's voice:

"I'll be home for Christmas. You can count on me…"

Lillian gasped. Francie and Carla clapped their hands over their mouths. David's jaw dropped and in spite of the scruffy beard, I could see his face turn pale.

I looked at all of them, not understanding their reaction.

"That's Dad's song," Jim said almost silently by my ear.

Of course. The song the family had grown so tired of every Christmas season, but that they were afraid to hear this year, because it brought back the raw pain of their loss.

Matthew continued to sing. He was standing near a

window. It was full dark outside, but the moon and stars were bright.

Jim knelt next to him. "Hey, pardner. Where'd you learn to sing that?

Matthew blinked and looked at Jim. "The trees."

"Trees?"

"The trees sing it to me." He looked around at everyone standing in the Christmas shop in total silence. "When I play with Grampa Harry's truck, the trees sing. Daisy listens too."

David was flustered. "You called him Grandpa Harry?"

Matthew looked at him, frowning. Then he turned to look outside again. "My Grampa Harry. In the trees."

I glanced to Francie's son, Joseph. He was the only known grandchild, the only person who would have referred to Harry as Grandpa. But Joseph had never been around Matthew until just a little while ago. And nobody here had taught Matthew the song.

"Honey," said Lillian, "maybe you learned that song at preschool."

I knew he hadn't. At preschool they were into the

big show stoppers like "Jingle Bells" and "Here Comes Santa Claus."

There's no way my four year old could have learned a relatively complicated song like "I'll Be Home for Christmas," when all the people he spent time with made sure the song was never played.

Unless, like me, you believe what Matthew says.

And unless, like me, you believe that there's more than a little magic in Serendipity, Indiana. Especially at Christmas.

The End...or is it The Beginning?

Did you like this story?

If so, please consider writing a review on your favorite

retailer's website. Thank you!

-Magdalena

Did you enjoy your time in Serendipity? Here's what is planned for 2015:

Book Two: EMILY'S DREAMS

Emily Kincaid's recovery after her auto accident astonished the doctors, but there are plenty of other surprises in store for Emily and those she loves—and will come to love.

Book Three: THE BLANK BOOK

Alice Williams is surviving widowhood, but must unlock the secrets of a mysterious blank book before she can confidently step into her future with a man she's afraid to love.

Book Four: THE ROAD NOT TAKEN

Francie Standish Carrington has some tough decisions to make, and a lot of questions about a past she thought she understood.

Book Five: THE RING

A fascinating man has stepped into Carla Standish's perfect life. He's brought a beautiful gift, lots of baggage, and a promise he may not be able to fulfill.

Book Six: A PIECE OF HER SOUL

Jacqueline has a special gift. She senses what is missing from people's souls, and helps them fill the void. After years of this highly emotional, exhausting work, she needs a break.

But the little cottage on a quiet street isn't quite the retreat she expected. Because there's a handsome police chief next door, and her sixth sense tells her he needs something. How she wishes that something was her...

Book Seven: CHRISTMAS WEDDING

The annual excitement of the season at Standish Christmas Tree Farm includes a wedding—and the kind of surprises you always expect in Serendipity, Indiana.

Sign up for her email newsletter at Magdalena's website, so you'll be one of the first to know what's new in Serendipity! www.magdalenascott.com

ABOUT THE AUTHOR

USA TODAY Bestselling Author Magdalena Scott writes sweet romance and women's fiction full of well-drawn characters and rich descriptions that may have you wishing you lived in one of her imaginary towns. Step into Magdalena's world for romance, drama, humor, mystery, and occasional bits of the inexplicable. Her stories also promise you a happy ending every time--a guarantee you won't find just everywhere. Magdalena is a lifelong resident of small town America, and shares her otherwise serene studio apartment with Attila, the Kitten from Heck.

Would you like to sign up for her newsletter, read her blog, or connect on social media? All the links are on her website: www.magdalenascott.com.